Christmas Parables

Unwrapping the Gift of Hope

by Terry Austin

Austin Brothers Publishing
www.christmasparablesbook.com

Austin Brothers
Publishing

Christmas Parables
Unwrapping the Gift of Hope
by Terry Austin

Art Work: Jeff and Andrea Austin
Book Design: Rick Wallace

Published by Austin Brothers Publishing
Keller, Texas

ISBN 978-0-9819023-0-2 ISBN

Christmas Parables
Unwrapping the Gift of Hope

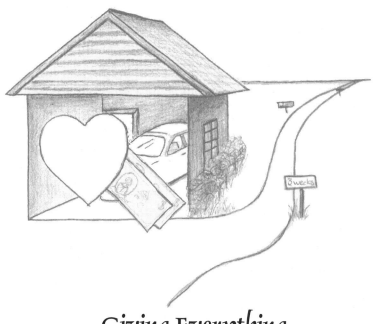

Giving Everything

Thanksgiving Day came to a merciful completion. The entire family went home well fed and exhausted. Everyone had been there long enough to get caught up on new news and rehash old stories, but not long enough to rub against each other the wrong way. Even though it would take Sandra a few days to return the house to its usual order, the final verdict was that it was a good day.

Grant was the last to leave after the festivities. It was always difficult to pull himself away from his children and return to his empty house. His daughter Sandra made it especially hard because she had many similar characteristics to her mother. From the way she added color to her face with cosmetics, to the way she spread holiday decorations around the house, everything reminded Grant of his former wife.

Being in her home was like thumbing through a scrapbook for Grant, highlighting the years that he and his wife had been together and shared the holidays. Too bad the majority of their marriage had been anything but a holiday. After a decade and a half of trying, they admitted failure and went separate ways.

His daughter Sandra, along with his sons Chris and Thomas, demonstrated that Grant's marriage wasn't a total disappointment. Each of them seemed to be happily married, or at least content enough, as they built their own families. Grant felt like a fortunate man with such a large, warm family.

Moving from Thanksgiving to Christmas requires a quick turnaround. It was going to be especially difficult this year because of so many other things going on with Grant. After years of workaholism, Grant had accumulated enough money to take early retirement. At least that is what he convinced himself that he was doing.

He made the retirement announcement to his children at the Thanksgiving table. They immediately started filling up his calendar, now that he would no longer be consumed with his work. It was a fun exercise, but Grant wasn't interested in anyone else's suggestions. He already had his own plans.

Becoming financially stable was not that difficult after the divorce. One of the perpetual conflicts that separated Grant and his wife was finances. She was a free spender and he was a frugal saver. Actually, to be more honest, his children would probably say that he was cheap. Being divorced allowed him to give himself completely to his work which resulted in the accumulation of a significant nest egg. Life is much easier when you only live for yourself.

Those who knew Grant might have been surprised to learn of his self-centered approach to life. He gave the impression of interest while listening to the stories of others. That is why the insurance business proved to be easy pickings for Grant. People trusted him, which allowed him to get the all important signature on an insurance application. Grant really did care. He was not just pretending. However, he had greater interest in the size of his commission.

After the divorce, he had time and incentive to commit himself totally to the task of making money. Obviously, he was no Warren Buffett, but he was making a six-figure income years before it was expected by everyone in the white-collar world.

Don't misunderstand, Grant was not totally selfish. From childhood he had been taught to give to the church and he did that dependably. In fact, the legalist within motivated him to be what his pastor called a "faithful tither." But his giving went beyond the bare minimum. Just last year, Grant donated an extra three thousand dollars for the new church building fund, and every Christmas for as long as he could remember, Grant wrote out a check for one hundred dollars to the Salvation Army. He knew that God had blessed him and he was willing to do his part.

In fact, this year was going to be special. He had already decided to double the one hundred dollar gift certificate that he gave to each of his children for Christmas. They would be surprised on Christmas morning when they tore open the accompanying card. Although he would never say anything, Grant hoped they would put the extra money away in a savings account.

Grant's life was about to change and he was ready. No more countless hours in the office or long weekends on the road. His time would be his own from now on. He had not told his children yet, but the deposit check on a new home on the edge of the lake had just cleared his account. He planned to spend the first six months of the New Year helping the builder make all the right choices. The fifty-seven years of his life were about to pay off in a big way.

Pulling his heavy wool coat from the closet, Grant kissed Sandra, hugged his two grandkids, said his goodbyes, and stepped out into the cold. The frigid air had not been a problem all day because everyone stayed in the house, close to the turkey and stuffing. As Grant walked to his car, wispy flakes of snow were falling helplessly to the ground. As he turned the ignition in his eight year old Honda, Grant anticipated being safe at home before the roads became a problem.

The five mile trip from Sandra's house to home was uneventful. Other than fidgeting with a slight discomfort in his chest, Grant spent the entire time dreaming about his new home on the lake. He was not worried about the physical discomfort. After all, he had eaten a hearty

Thanksgiving meal, complete with an extra piece of pumpkin pie just a few minutes before he left.

However, the night did not end as you might expect. If Grant were telling the story he would not be able to recount any of the details. The only thing he knew for sure was that he woke up the next morning in the hospital. The tightness in his chest was not pumpkin pie. The evening had included severe pain, ambulance sirens, and emergency surgery to repair his heart. It is unnecessary to tell you that Grant's plans for the holidays were changed.

But, not only were his plans modified. When Grant woke up from surgery, something within him was different. It might be accurate to say that Grant's heart was repaired in more ways than one.

Let me clarify. His heart was really not repaired. In fact, the surgery did little more than keep him from dying that night in the emergency room. His physical problem could not be fixed. Grant was barely awake from the anesthetic when he heard a doctor say that he was living on borrowed time and he better get his affairs in order. Well, that's not the words used by the doctor, but that is the message Grant heard.

One thing the doctor did say was, "You might be able to share Christmas with your family."

Not even New Years! Just a meager month!

It is amazing how you can go from preparing for the second half of your life, to facing the final month of your life so quickly. It is hard to say if time means nothing, or if time means everything.

When he heard the devastating news from the doctors, Grant's mind seemed to freeze solid; he couldn't absorb anything.

All of his children were in the room as the doctor spoke. Chris had a promising career. He had inherited his father's frugality, and was well on his way to providing well for his family. Thomas was still young, or so it seemed. It was three years since college graduation and he was still seeking a permanent direction. The boys also had their older sister Sandra. As long as she was around, Grant never worried. She had the ability to handle any situation and solve every problem.

Besides, even though Grant and his ex-wife did not have a relationship, she was still a big part of their lives. Even if Grant passed on at such a young age, the children would be fine.

There is something about sharing a hospital room with someone. Having to face mortality knowing that a virtual stranger is in the same room, separated only by a pale hospital curtain, that tends to move you further in the relationship than normal. In fact, Grant did not even have time to meet his roommate before hearing the dark news from his doctor.

Reggie, the roommate, was a hardy looking young husband and father who had been scraped from the road following a bloody automobile wreck. After working a second shift of overtime in order to have more Christmas money, Reggie stopped at a small pub for a few drinks before going home. His late night drive home was interrupted by an out-of-control SUV that plowed into the side of Reggie's pickup. Although the accident was not Reggie's fault, perhaps if he had skipped the beers and been clear headed, he could have taken evasive measures.

When Grant was finally able to pull himself together enough to speak to Reggie, he also met Reggie's wife Janet and their energetic three-year-old Deion. His injuries were not life-threatening, but his right leg was severely crushed, and he was facing a series of surgeries to return him back to mobility. In spite of the fact that Grant's condition was terminal, he would actually be leaving the hospital much quicker than Reggie.

Recovering from surgery, Grant was not lacking for time to think about his situation. A bland, bright hospital room with tiled floors, brightly painted walls, and the constant hum of medical equipment, was not the ideal place to ponder eternal matters. When he tired of his thoughts and despair, Grant would look to Reggie for conversation and distraction.

Reggie was only a few years older than Grant's son, Thomas, which at least gave them some common experiences to discuss. With his insurance background, one of the natural questions Grant asked was about insurance. He learned that Reggie and his family had no insurance. Even worse, the driver of the SUV was also without coverage.

From a financial perspective, Reggie's future was no less tenuous than Grant's. Reggie's family lived only two paychecks away from bankruptcy, and Reggie could easily miss six months of work while waiting for his leg to heal. Being rescued by family was not an option, so it appeared they were alone with little hope. As you might imagine, there was very little laughing in room four fifteen.

The second night in the hospital was off to a better start for Grant, but it did not last. He fell into a deep sleep, primarily from exhaustion and medication. However, his slumber was interrupted by an unsettling dream. At least Grant hoped it had been a dream. Perhaps it was something more.

He awoke with a vague memory of a sleep induced vision, an encounter with Jesus. It was not some type of Pentecostal trance or hypnotic trick. It was a dream, neither more nor less real than any of the other thousands of dreams Grant had experienced over his lifetime.

If you were to ask Grant, and you would have to ask because he would not bring up the subject, he would tell you that he is a man of faith. He spent his childhood Sundays in church, developing a habit that continued his whole life. Along the way he had some significant religious experiences, although they had become rather rare since his marriage dissipated. But, dreams of conversations with Jesus were not a part of his experience. Given his hospital induced, fragile emotional condition, Grant was unnerved.

As he tried to clear his mind, Grant kept hearing the voice of Jesus asking, "Now, who will own what you have prepared?"

The question left Grant restless throughout the early morning. Even as the nurses and orderlies began their usual symptom checking, room cleaning, and medication disbursement, the question was foremost in Grant's mind.

Even though he ate a good breakfast, his first real meal since Thanksgiving dinner at Sandra's house, he could not shake the words of his night visitor.

It must have been a coincidence that morning when the first visitor was Rev. Russell, the long tenured pastor of Grant's church. Frank Russell was the kind of man who made everyone comfortable. He was rather old fashioned, wearing a dark suit everyday and keeping his gray hair cropped short. Everyone liked him because he liked everyone. Many at the church would say he was the ideal pastor. He had been in the community so long that he knew every secret, yet people still trusted him.

Grant and Rev. Russell had never had a genuinely serious conversation about feelings and spiritual problems. Grant was not the kind of man who discussed those things with anyone. But, he was always confident if he ever had a need for such a conversation, Rev. Russell would be the one. Now, here he was, standing at the foot of Grant's hospital bed, wearing his customary blue suit and white shirt, holding a worn dark leather Bible in his left hand and extending his right hand for a shake.

"Grant, how are you doing?" asked Rev. Russell, not being aware of the terrible news about Grant's future.

Grabbing the preacher's hand, Grant replied sincerely, "Rev. Russell, I am so glad to see you! Sit down. We need to talk."

For the next few moments, Grant rehashed the experience, including his family Thanksgiving, emergency surgery, and frightening prognosis from the doctor. It was obvious that Rev. Russell was deeply saddened by Grant's ordeal and tragic future.

When it was time for him to speak, Rev. Russell said, "Grant, I am so sorry. What can I do to help?"

"I was hoping you would ask that," responded Grant.

He then launched into a detailed description of his restless night, recalling as many details from the dream as possible. Then he asked for Rev. Russell's help. "The question by Jesus, 'Now who will own what you have prepared?' What does it mean?"

"I don't know, Grant," said Rev. Russell in a tentative voice. "I'm certainly no expert on dreams. However, I do recognize those words from the Bible."

Speaking as a man who had faithfully read the book every morning of his life, he added, "I recognize the words as being in one of Jesus' parables. Do you remember the story of the farmer who built new barns when he made a bunch of money? He thought he had everything he needed since he was rich, but then he found out he was going to die that night. That's when he was asked, 'Now who will own what you have prepared?' But, I don't know what that means for you."

Rev. Russell was unaware of Grant's financial situation, so of course he didn't know what it meant. But, as soon as the minister spoke, Grant knew exactly what the words meant. It was one of those "eureka" moments that happen seldom in life.

After his pastor left the hospital, Grant began the wrestling process in his mind. Being confident of what he should do did not necessarily give him the ability to do it. He had spent so much time, more than half his life, accumulating. Now, he had these thoughts of giving it all away. This was not an emotional response caused by a near death, or even an approaching death experience. Grant thought this might be the right thing to do.

Like any normal parent, he had given thought over the years to leaving an inheritance, but he never expected it to actually happen. It was always one of those eventual realities that was still a long time away. Now, here it was, as close and uncomfortable as a disheveled stranger in an elevator.

Grant always assumed he would simply divide his assets among his children, which seemed the fairest thing to do. As they grew older and established their own families, it was obvious they did not really need the money, but Grant had never given any thought of doing anything else.

As doctors and nurses came and went throughout the day, Grant was distracted by Jesus' thorny question. He barely heard his doctor's report that healing from surgery was progressing well and that he would be able to go home on Monday morning. He tried to focus as they presented the medicine regimen he would need to follow.

Finally, late on Sunday afternoon, Grant resolved the issue. He had been a fool for wasting so much time worrying about his finances. After a lifetime of accumulating, providing for his family, giving to his church, and carefully saving his money, it was ridiculous to think about giving it all away now. Especially now when his future was so bleak. He was sure there would be enormous medical expenses and unexpected situations that would require everything he had saved. Once he returned to the comfort of his home, Grant knew that his thinking would return to normal and he could forget this foolish notion of giving everything away.

On Monday morning, Grant awoke with a tinge of excitement. He was going home. Sandra arrived early with fresh clothes to wear. Once all the tubes and sensors were removed, Grant quickly dressed and prepared to leave. He caught himself just before stepping into the hall. He needed to tell Reggie goodbye.

Poking his head through the curtain that separated their beds, Grant said, "Reggie, I'm leaving. I hope your leg heals quickly and you get out of this joint soon!"

"Thanks Grant," Reggie sounded dejected as he spoke. "I'm sure my leg will be fine. I just hope I still have a family and a place to go when it is."

Grant knew the feeling of hopelessness, given his current physical condition, but here was a young man with his whole life in front of him who expressed the same hopelessness. The melancholy sound of Reggie's words would interfere with Grant's thinking for the rest of the day.

Reggie and his family had a future, but very few resources or opportunities. Grant was returning to a nice home and an abundant bank account, but no future. That pesky question by Jesus began replaying in his mind once again, "Now who will own what you have prepared?"

The ride home was quiet. Conversation was difficult. They were both preoccupied-Sandra with thoughts of losing her father and Grant with thoughts of giving away all of his stuff.

Grant was not surprised to find his house prepared to receive a man freshly home from a stay in the hospital. Brenda took care of everything. If the doctor was correct and he had a month at the most, there would be no need to leave the house again. Grant wasn't sure what he would feel like doing, but he was confident that he did not want to spend the final month of life confined like a prisoner under house arrest.

While sitting at the table eating lunch, Grant decided to share his dream and thoughts with Sandra, confident that her level-headed thinking would help him get this wild idea in better perspective. After intently listening she carefully chose her words. Without using the word "crazy," she essentially told her father that he was crazy.

No one in their right mind would just give everything away. Besides, with his illness, Grant didn't know what kind of medical expenses he might have. Also, Sandra was unwilling to admit that the doctor was absolutely correct. She still had hope that her father's body would heal and he would live a long time. If that happened, he would need his money.

Sandra did exactly what Grant hoped would happen. She clearly expressed every objection to his notion of giving. It was good to hear it from someone else; at least he knew he was not just being selfish. Once again, Grant thought he could rest easy. Instead of wasting valuable energy on giving, he could now focus his attention on getting well.

After Sandra left, Grant sat down at his desk to review the

mail that had accumulated during his hospital stay. It would only take a few minutes to sort out the important items from the piles of junk, and then he would take an afternoon nap.

He had never noticed before, but Grant was surprised to discover the large number of worthy organizations that considered him a potential donor. He knew that the Christmas season was a big time for fund raising, and everyone was giving it their best shot. He felt like the bulls eye.

But, it gave him an idea. Perhaps if he gave generously to these folks, the crazy notion of giving everything would disappear from his mind. After all, what God was trying to tell him was that he needed to be a little more generous. He could accept that without giving up everything.

Grant pulled his checkbook from the top desk drawer and began to wade through the postal solicitations. There were eight organizations that he recognized. His first thought was to give them each a hundred dollars, but he instinctly knew that would not be enough to clear his mind. So, he wrote out eight checks for a thousand dollars apiece, slid them in the return envelopes, and prepared them for tomorrow's mail.

His grand generosity made Grant feel wonderful. In fact, he had not felt this good in years. Maybe Rev. Russell had been on to something all these years when he told the congregation that it is more blessed to give than to receive. Grant crawled into bed for his nap, confident that he had accomplished what his dream had been trying to tell him.

Grant was roused from a deep sleep by an electronic ring. It took several seconds to get his wits, roll over on his left side, and grab the phone. When he spoke, a rather weak hello came from his mouth.

"Grant, is that you," asked the voice in Grant's ear.

"Yes," said Grant, "Who is this?"

"Grant, this is Reggie, from the hospital. Remember me?"

"Of course I do, Reggie. It's only been a few hours," replied Grant.

"I should have thought of this earlier," Reggie said as the excitement began to build in his voice. "I know you are a successful man and you probably know a bunch of people. I was wondering, do you know anyone who might give Janet a job? We have to do something and I'm not going to be able to work and we've got all these bills and Christmas is coming... We have to do something and I was hoping maybe you could help!"

This was the first time Grant had ever been asked directly for help by anyone except one of his children. He felt sorry for Reggie and Janet, but he was not sure what he could do. Grant asked Reggie a few questions about Janet's work experience and skills and then promised that he would try to do something, although he had no idea of what that might be.

Hanging up the phone did not silence the desperation that Grant heard in Reggie's voice. He knew he had do something. Besides, that nagging voice from his dream returned, but now it had the same vocal intonation as Reggie. Writing the checks earlier in the afternoon only silenced the voice long enough for Grant to take a short nap. He was not off the hook yet.

The more Grant thought about Reggie's need, the more he realized how big a task he faced. This young family needed everything. He could not work, they were facing enormous hospital bills, and they would lose their house in a few months. It would not be enough to just buy them a few Christmas gifts.

Another sleepless night awaited Grant. He wanted to get this issue resolved so it would not ruin the final month of his life. Like a skilled lawyer, Grant carefully evaluated both sides of the issue, and like a meticulous jury he weighed the evidence.

As he crawled out of bed Wednesday morning, Grant had made his decision. He was resolved to give everything away. The next few weeks would be spent making decisions on who would receive all his money. He was committed to giving it all away. Grant couldn't wait to get to the hospital and share his plans with Reggie, because that is where it would all begin.

Grant was glad that Janet was at the hospital when he arrived so he could tell both of them his plan. He was really crawling out on a limb, but he was as excited as a child in an amusement park. He told them how he would take care of all of Reggie's medical expenses, but that was just the beginning. He was also going to give them his house and provide enough so Reggie would not have to worry about working until he was physically able. It took Grant some time to convince Reggie that he was not hallucinating.

Grant did not remember walking to his car after he left Reggie's hospital room. He was flooded with joy, unlike anything he had ever experienced. If he had only known that giving was this exciting, he would have started a long time ago.

It took nearly the entire month for Grant to give everything away. It was not as easy as it sounds. It was not like he could just walk through the mall and hand out hundred dollar bills, although he did do that one afternoon. When he retired he had assets totaling nearly two million dollars. The experience was so amazing and fulfilling that he sometimes forgot that he was dying.

But his body did not forget. By Christmas Eve, it was apparent that the doctor had made an accurate prediction. Grant was tired and weak. Yet, he approached the end of life with an amazing confidence for a fifty-seven year old-he had accomplished what God had called him to do. He had learned that all those years of making money were simply preparation for the final month of his life when he could give it away.

After a very pleasant Christmas Eve with his family, Grant went to bed, unaware that one more dream was waiting. Once again he heard a message from one that he perceived to be Jesus. It simply said, "Well done, good and faithful servant."

A Misunderstood Servant

Christmas is a difficult time for me. How would you like to be portrayed as the bad guy, the man who didn't care? People talk as if they know a great deal about me but they really don't know anything. Every church pageant and school play requires someone to don an old bathrobe and sandals, put on an angry scowl, and recite lines that I never said.

You think you know me well because you have heard the Christmas story all your life. You are so familiar with the story that you don't really pay attention as it's read. You know about the shepherds, the Magi from the East, Joseph and his dear wife Mary, and of course, the baby Jesus. You've seen so many nativity-recreations, complete with cows and sheep, that you think you know everything.

Other than Herod, I am the only villain in the story. I have been labeled as cold, heartless, uncaring, and mean. All of these slanderous accusations have come from believers, many of them who claim to take the Scripture very seriously. The truth is that I am never mentioned in the Bible.

Go ahead! Read the story again. You can wear out the pages with your eyes but you will never see a word about an Innkeeper. In spite of my absence from the holy writ, you have all thought of me as a pitiless profiteer who forced a pregnant woman to sleep in a cold, smelly barn.

I don't know where the notion started, but it is far from the truth. Listen carefully; I am not disputing that Jesus was born in a stable, nor the fact that the inn was filled for the night. My concern is to set the record straight about my actions on that sacred night. Perhaps the best way is to simply tell you what happened as I remember the details.

Bethlehem was a small village, located just a few miles from the busyness of Jerusalem. Other than the fact that it was the hometown of the great King David, there was nothing else significant about the town. I was the local innkeeper. You can be assured that it was not an occupation I pursued. My intentions were to become an artisan. I had a knack for creating beautiful jewelry. My plan was to produce enough so I could open a small booth in the Jerusalem market.

If you have lived as long as I, you too have discovered that plans do not always work out.

My father was a skilled carpenter. He built a house that was one of the most luxurious in Bethlehem; some boasted that it was the finest house outside of Jerusalem. His reputation with a knife and a chisel were legendary and he had more business than he and I, his only son, could handle. The hard work of cutting and shaping lumber was not to my liking. I longed for the day when I was old enough to make my fortune as a jeweler.

One hot summer afternoon, father and I were in the shop cutting lumber. Father's hand slipped and his knife cut a long gash in his left arm. I helped him into the house and mother finally stopped the bleeding. For several days we thought he was going to die. We were terrified.

After more than two weeks of lying in bed, father finally started to regain his strength. It was apparent that he was going to live but it was also obvious that he would not be able to use his arm. In our world, there was not much work for a one-armed carpenter.

I tried to keep the carpentry business running but I was too young and inexperienced. All of the money that my parents had saved was soon gone. The one resource that remained was our beautiful, large house.

My father decided that the best way to continue to provide for his family was to turn our house into an inn for travelers. That meant the whole family would have to work. At first it was exciting, welcoming weary travelers into our home. We heard tales from those who had seen the world and my dream of being a jeweler in Jerusalem expanded to the far reaches of the earth.

However, the excitement of running an inn soon wore off. Travelers are not always the best of citizens and we lost many of our possessions to thieves. Often, the sick were left at our doorstep to care for. It was hard work with very little profit.

My father died when I was still a very young man. The responsibility of providing for the family fell upon my shoulders. Instead of traveling the world, marketing jewelry, I found myself as an overworked innkeeper in the insignificant village of Bethlehem. My dreams died painfully.

I ran that inn for nearly thirty years. I raised my own family in the same house, still large, but no longer very beautiful.

When Caesar Augustus sent out the proclamation for a census, it turned our world upside down. It was like a great homecoming. Many who had been born and raised in our little village returned for the registration. For many weeks, reunions were happening in almost every home.

Work at the inn heightened to a frantic pace. We began early every morning and labored until late into the night. It was good to see old friends, but there was little time to converse. Day after day, every room in our house was filled with guests. The profits were good but I'm not sure they were enough to compensate for the cost to my family and our health.

The night that you are most interested in was at the end

of a very hectic stretch. The inn was totally filled with travelers; in fact, late in the afternoon I began turning away potential customers. There was just no place for anyone to stay.

We finally completed all the chores and locked the front door for the night. I sat on the mattress next to my beloved Naomi, anticipating a short but restful night. Hard work always brings good rest at the end of the day.

We were startled to hear a hard pounding on the door. It was already late and I could not imagine who would be demanding to be let in at this time of the night. Opening the door after it has been closed for the night is no small chore. I stood at the door and shouted that the inn was full.

The man on the outside would not give up. He kept pounding and pleading that I open the door. He spoke of his wife and her need for help. Against my initial inclination and the pleadings of Naomi, I lifted the bolt and opened the door. My plan was to express my concern for their need and then suggest that they move on to Jerusalem. There were no more beds in Bethlehem.

I swung the door open but before I could utter a word, the man started talking. He said, "Kind sir, are you Nathan?"

I was startled that this stranger knew my name. "Yes," I stammered, "My name is Nathan. How do you know me?"

"My name is Joseph," he replied, "I am the son of Jacob who now lives in Nazareth. He was your friend when you were children."

I began to rummage through my memory to a time nearly forty years earlier. I remembered a Jacob who had moved away with his family. We had been friends because his father was also a carpenter. We played in the fields together and we often worked together in our fathers' shops to make the time go faster.

Now his son stood before me, asking for help. He spoke of their journey from Nazareth that had taken more than a week. His young wife Mary was expecting a child, and she was very, very tired from the trip. As he told his story, I tried to think how we could help this young family.

I stepped into the house to get Naomi; perhaps she had an idea of how to provide for Joseph and Mary. Every corner of the inn was filled with weary travelers and it was deep enough into the night that they were all asleep. I suggested that we give up our bed for the night. However, Naomi reminded me that the others would be up early in the morning, requesting the help of the innkeeper. That would mean a very short night for the soon-to-be mother.

We both had the thought at the same time and in unison we said, "Stable!" Now, before you become disdainful and ask, "How can you put them in the barn?" let me explain my actions.

You think that a stable is a drafty, filthy, dilapidated structure, filled with cows and sheep. That is not how I would describe our stable. Our house was located on the edge of the village and just a short walk from our front door was the stable. It was really a cave, a shallow cutout in a large rock on the outskirts of town.

During the summer when the evenings were hot, Naomi and I often slept in the stable because it was cool. The night when Joseph and Mary arrived was in the spring, so the shepherds had all the sheep in the fields. There was no livestock in the stable, only clean, dry straw. We chose the stable because it was cool and quiet, the ideal place for a good night's rest.

We had no idea that Mary would give birth to the child on that very night. Our plan was to provide the finest room in the inn as soon as it became available the next day. I did not turn them out in the cold. I gave them the very best that I had.

You already know that it turned into an incredible night. The baby boy was born just a few short hours after we got Mary comfortably settled in the stable. My wife helped with the birth but there was really not much to do. Everything went so smoothly that it was almost as if it had been planned to happen precisely as it did.

We were certainly surprised when the shepherds came in from the fields unexpectedly. They spoke of singing angels directing them to the stable. It is rare indeed for a shepherd to leave his flock in the field during the middle of the night. It was truly an incredible happening.

Many of the events of that night never did make sense until years later when I heard the amazing stories about Jesus of Nazareth. It seems that the Messiah, God's own Son, had been born in my stable.

As I have contemplated the events of that evening, I realize that God used me as a small part of His plan.

I didn't have very much. In fact, all I had was an empty stable. However, it was the very best that I could possibly do, and when I gave the very best that I had, God used it to give the very best that He had.

The Greatest Christmas Gift

Leaving church on Sunday morning with a new outlook on life was not a common experience for Walter. He normally ended the hour of worship with a growling stomach and acute anxiety that he had missed the opening kickoff. But, today was different. Something the preacher said captured his attention.

He didn't mind going to church, even though he would not classify himself as a steadfast believer. Walter had no doubts about the existence of God, and he rarely disagreed with anything spoken from the pulpit; he just had other interests. He enjoyed church because he loved sitting next to Sally. She was the love of his life, the apple of his eye, and every other cliché you can think of. More often than not, they would even hold hands for a good portion of the hour.

The amazing thing of Walter's strong affection for Sally is that they were not young teenagers in love. Walter and Sally had been married for forty-two years. Yet, he was just as eager to sit at her side as he had been when they first met as college freshmen. The years had brought them closer. In fact, since Walter retired six months ago, they spent most of their time together and he had never been happier.

It was the first Sunday of Advent, a time that Walter always enjoyed. He loved everything about Christmas, especially the gifts. For Walter, giving a present was a process, including shopping, wrapping, hiding, and opening. His greatest joy every Christmas morning was to watch expressions as family and friends opened the gift he meticulously picked for them. For Walter, the first Sunday of Advent was the signal that Christmas was almost here.

The sermon by Rev. Wilson was about the gift of God that we celebrate at Christmas. He pounded home the notion that God's gift was the greatest ever. He defined that gift as loving those who are unlovable. Rev. Wilson was not known for his oratory skills, but whenever he worked at it, he could be as convincing as any car salesman pushing an extended warranty.

Whatever he said on Sunday, he certainly captured Walter's attention. In spite of the fact that Walter had been attending church for decades and that he had heard hundreds of Christmas sermons, something about the words of Rev. Wilson captured his interest. Like a child entering a toy store, Walter's mind was racing with possibilities.

He decided that Christmas was about loving the unlovable. This was revolutionary to Walter. He had spent his whole life giving to those he loved. He could not remember ever giving a present to someone who was unlovable. He had never even given it a moment's thought.

Walter and Sally put on their coats as they walked toward the church foyer. Leaving church was always tedious for Walter because Sally liked to stop and visit with too many people. She was accustomed to Walter tugging on her sleeve like bored child. On this Sunday, Walter walked off and left Sally. He was in a hurry to speak to Rev. Wilson.

Waiting his turn in the line with the complimenters and complainers, Walter finally reached the preacher. Walter stretched out both arms and grabbed the Reverend's hand.

"Pastor, you really spoke to me today," he blurted out as he shook the minister's hand like a rag doll.

"Thank you, Walter," said Rev. Wilson in a tentative voice, "I was just trying to say what God laid on my heart." He was somewhat stunned because he did not remember his words ever having had an impact on Walter before.

Almost before Rev. Wilson finished his sentence, Walter said, "Pastor, I've got an idea about Christmas. You convinced me that Christmas is about loving the unlovable. That's what I am going to do!"

Not sure what Walter had in mind, Rev. Wilson said,

"That's good to hear, Walter. It's always good to know that someone is listening when I preach."

"Pastor, this is my plan. I'm going to find the most unlovable person in town, and I'm going to love them. That will be my Christmas present to them."

You could still hear some skepticism, or perhaps it was simply reservation in Rev. Wilson's voice, "That's great, Walter. I'll be glad to help. Just let me know what I can do."

Walter didn't hear the last few words because he had already turned to look for Sally. She was finishing her conversation as Walter seized her arm and escorted her out the front door toward the parking lot.

As they walked toward the car, Walter shared his idea with Sally. He knew she would love it. She always supported Walter in everything he did. However, she also knew that sometimes Walter got distracted before his plans were finished, so she didn't get too caught up with his excitement. She was more interested in getting Sunday dinner on the table because she had plans with the grandchildren for the afternoon.

Walter and Sally frequently enjoyed the company of their three grandchildren. Sally's plan for the day was to take Beth and Amy to a new outlet store that specialized in their favorite clothing. The girls, consumer-trained pre-teens, were excited because they knew Grandma could not resist buying them stuff.

After lunch, Walter disappeared to his workroom behind the garage. It was where he did his best thinking, and his plan to find the most unlovable person in town required some thought. He heard his son and daughter-in-law, Rob and Marcia, in the house; they brought the girls over to go shopping with Grandma. Walter was so excited about his plan that he hurried into the kitchen to tell them all about it.

Rob and Marcia began to throw out names of unlovable people, but they were mostly folks that Walter barely knew. It seems that everyone has their own set of disagreeable acquaintances. Everyone had a good time talking about all their bad experiences, but the suggestions were of no help to Walter. He decided that he would have to do his own research. It wasn't enough to love someone else's unlovable person.

While Sally was out shopping, Walter began putting together his list of unlovables. He did not want to go too far into the past, because he needed someone that was nearby; someone that he could love. Of course, he first thought about a homeless person living on the streets and in the shelters downtown. A man reeking of body odor and bad breath is certainly difficult to love. Walter didn't know any homeless people, and it is hard to love someone if you don't even know them.

So, he decided to expand his list. One of the first names to come to mind was Al Barnes. He worked with Al for nearly fifteen years. Walter tried to get along with him, but it was impossible. Walter was in sales and Al was in accounting. Al thought his job description included making everyone miserable. He questioned every item on every expense report. If you ever lost a receipt, it was easier to pay it yourself than to convince Al that it was a legitimate expense.

Al constantly belittled employees for the way they lived. When anyone parked a new car in the parking lot, Al would go out of his way to inform them that they purchased the wrong model, or paid too much for useless accessories. Instead of complimenting a new suit, Al would ask where you bought it and then call you stupid for shopping in such an expensive store. He even had the nerve to criticize Walter for throwing away his lunch sack instead of folding it up and using it again.

Everyone at the company hated Al. He was one of the reasons Walter retired as early as he did. Whenever he had regrets about not working longer, Walter remembered Al and his love for retirement was rekindled. Al might be more unlovable than any homeless person in the city.

Since he already had a list going, Walter decided to add another name, just in case. This one was easy—Sally's cousin, Mark. Mark was the family plague. Everyone pretended that he didn't exist because he was an embarrassment. In and out of jail, seldom employed, always needing money, or to borrow the car, or a place to stay, he had been married a couple of times, but Walter wasn't sure exactly how many.

Walter certainly did not hate Mark, he barely knew him. He had no feelings one way or the other. However, he knew from conversations and family gatherings that there was nothing good about Mark. Any bad quality you could name, Mark had it. He was certainly high up on everyone's unlovable list.

Walter had enough names. Now, it was time to devise a plan. It was already getting late on Sunday afternoon; Sally and the grandkids would be home soon, so Walter decided to wait until tomorrow. He would get out in the morning and start an adventure that he expected to make his most memorable Christmas. The determination that motivated him as soon as he heard Rev. Wilson's words had not waned.

The air was crisp and cold when Walter walked out the front door on Monday morning. He had an extra jump in his step this morning, because he was out to do God's work. The plan was to approach someone at one of the city's two homeless shelters downtown. He would ask around and find the most unlovable of the regulars.   He planned to spend a few days, get to know the man, buy him some presents, and really demonstrate love. It was a good plan, but he would soon discover, it was not that easy.

At the Washington Street Shelter, Walter went straight to the Director's office and introduced himself to Saul Fielder. Even though Saul was somewhat skeptical of Walter's plan, he saw the benefit of getting someone else involved with the ministry. He immediately thought of Ernest.

Ernest had already left the shelter after breakfast and the morning devotionals, but Saul Fielder told Walter exactly where he would find him. "Look on 5th Street, next to the library," he said. "He will be sitting on one of the benches, cussing at everyone who walks by."

Walter didn't like the sound of that. It sounded like he had found the most unlovable person in town. Walter pulled the lapels of his coat up under his neck and headed out the door of the shelter. The library was only two blocks away, so he left the car parked on the street.

Sure enough, Ernest was easy to find. Walter stood and watched for ten or fifteen minutes, as Ernest verbally berated everyone who walked into or out of the building. This was going to be difficult, but Walter was more determined than ever.

He took a deep breath and walked straight toward Ernest. When Ernest saw him coming, he was surprised, because nobody ever walked close by. Everyone else went out of their way to avoid any contact with him.

"What do you want?" he sneered, as Walter got close.

"Nothing, I just want to introduce myself and talk for a minute."

Ernest must have sensed the sincerity in Walter's voice because he chose to allow Walter to sit on the bench next to him. I'm not going to record their conversation, because it was filled with words that I have no business writing and you have no business reading. Let me just say, it was an enlightening discussion.

They talked for a long time before Ernest allowed Walter to purchase coffee. As they sat in the café, Ernest began to open up about himself. Through the profanity and ramblings, Walter was able to piece together why Ernest was so angry. It started three decades ago when Ernest was a newlywed. His wife was shot and killed during a robbery. The prosecutors botched the case and the killer avoided punishment. Ernest was so angry that he took matters into his own hands and nearly beat the young man to death. As a result, Ernest spent ten years in prison.

Drugs, alcohol, abandonment, and loneliness all contributed to his current anger. He chose to live on the streets because he didn't care about himself. The only goal he had for his life was to make others feel his wrath.

Walter and Ernest talked for an hour and a half. When they were finished, Ernest returned to the library and Walter drove home. He knew that this was the calling he heard in church on Sunday morning. Every morning for the next week, Walter and Earnest had coffee together and talked. By the end of the week, Earnest was no longer unlovable; at least to Walter. He was only unlovable to those who didn't know him.

Back to the drawing board! He would have to keep looking for someone who was unlovable. The second name on his list was Al Barnes from the office. Walter had no doubt that Al would meet all the qualifications of an unlovable subject.

Walter drove up to his old office building. It brought back a flood of memories, most of them pleasant. When he remembered he was there to see Al, the pleasant memories disappeared. As he entered the building, he greeted a few old friends along the way, but he did not want to be distracted from the task at hand. He made a straight line for Al's office. As usual, the door was closed. Al never liked anyone walking into his office unannounced so he kept the door shut.

Walter tapped on the door, and when he heard a grumble from inside, he slowly pushed it open. There was Al, sitting behind the desk as his fingers danced across the computer keyboard.

"Hey Al, its me, Walter," he said tentatively. He suddenly realized that he had failed to plan the conversation. Here he was in Al's office and he had no idea what to say.

"Walter, I haven't seen you in a long time," responded Al with surprise, "How's retirement?"

The next few minutes were consumed with inane chatter. At least it gave Walter some time to plan a strategy. He knew that he would soon have to explain why he was in Al's office.

Sure enough, here it came. "Why are you here, Walter?" Al spoke with his usual blunt manner.

Walter knew that Al liked to get to the point, so he decided to do just that. "I realized that during all the years we worked together, I never took the time to get to know you. I want to take you to lunch to say I'm sorry and to try and make up for being inconsiderate."

"What do you really want?" quizzed Al skeptically.

"Seriously, I feel bad that you and I never even tried to be friends, and I want to apologize."

Al was extremely hesitant. "You're not going to try and sign me up for Amway, or something like that, are you?"

Walter was eventually able to convince Al that he was sincere. The closer was when he assured Al that he was paying for lunch. They went to the Bluebonnet Diner. Walter chose that place because it was unlikely that they would be interrupted by anyone they knew and the prices were reasonable, which would impress Al.

Their conversation started slowly. It takes some time to develop trust, but Walter was determined to learn everything he could about this unlovable man. By the time the waitress brought coffee at the conclusion of the meal, Walter and Al were into serious conversation. It seems that Al was not as unapproachable as everyone thought.

Once again, Walter was able to piece together the story of an unlovable man. Al's wife, Sarah, had multiple sclerosis, a battle she had fought since they were a young couple. The expensive medicine and frequent hospital stays consumed all of their financial resources. Al, who was frugal by nature, had to keep the family on a very strict budget, just to keep up with their obligations. The combination of Sarah's health and the financial struggles had turned Al into a tired, frustrated, and lonely man. Rather than talking about his problems and seeking a friend for support, Al chose the opposite approach and pushed everyone away, wanting to appear self-sufficient.

As Al's story unfolded, Walter realized that he was not unlovable—just misunderstood. He felt guilty for not having made the effort to get to know Al. If everyone at the office knew the struggles Al and his wife faced, they would all be eager to help. Walter still knew enough people at the office that his plan of action came to him quickly. He would reintroduce Al to the others in the office, and their attitudes would immediately change. That is precisely what happened over the next few days.

Although Walter was feeling good about his new relationship with Ernest and Al, he was not any closer to his goal of loving the most unlovable person in town. He thought the hard part would be loving the person, not finding the person. So far, he hadn't found anyone who was unlovable.

He still had Sally's cousin Mark on his list. He must be the one. Once he had the opportunity to spend some time with Mark, Walter expected he would understand why everyone in the family hated him.

That opportunity never came. It was Saturday morning, nearly two weeks after Walter's divine revelation. The plan for the day was to try to locate Mark. His whereabouts was usually unknown, except when he showed up with his hand out. Walter had a short list of places where he might be able to locate the elusive cousin.

Sally had a much more pleasant day planned. She and Justin, their youngest grandchild, went to see the latest kid's movie and then had pizza. Walter wanted to go with them, but he was obsessed with completing his project. He would not be able to rest until the job was done.

Walter's day was unproductive. All of his leads about Mark proved to be stale. He drove home discouraged, looking forward to spending time with Sally and Justin. As he pulled into the driveway, he was surprised that Sally's car was not there. They must be having ice cream with their pizza, he thought. He went into the house and stretched out in his recliner, seeking to revitalize his discouraged mood.

He had almost dozed off when he was startled by the doorbell. Sally must have misplaced her key. Walter stood up and stretched before walking to the front door. He was prepared for Justin to leap into Grandpa's arms when he opened the door. He was caught off guard to find someone else on the front porch.

It was Rev. Wilson standing next to a police officer. "Pastor, I'm surprised to see you on Saturday. Don't worry; I'm planning to be in church tomorrow!"

He could tell immediately that this was not one of Rev. Wilson's typical pastoral visits. "Walter, we need to come in and talk. I'm afraid we have some news," Rev. Wilson spoke as he grabbed Walter's arm and escorted him back into the living room.

Walter was already starting to feel stunned; he knew this was not good news. Rev. Wilson, with a calm, confident voice, said, "Walter, I am so sorry. There has been a terrible accident, a car accident. Sally and Justin were involved. I don't know how to say this-it was terrible. Both Sally and Justin are gone."

Although Rev. Wilson never used the word dead, Walter knew. Everything that happened for the next several hours was a blur. Walter submitted himself to those around him. Family and friends appeared. All of his physical needs were met, decisions were made, and hugs were shared. Walter fought through the tears and tried to be responsive, but he had nothing to say. He had never felt so numb in his life.

Sally, the love of his life, his best friend, his supporter and encourager, was gone. She was his reason for living. Without Sally, his life had no purpose. He had no incentive to get up in the morning or go to bed at night. He could throw away his calendar because without Sally, every day was empty. The only thing he knew for sure was that his life was now meaningless.

As you know, Water was not the first, nor the last, to lose the most significant person in his life. He survived. Eventually. Christmas came and went; he didn't even remember it. Winter turned into spring. By early May, Walter's numbness was turning back into feelings, and he was able to return to normal living-at least as normal as his life would ever be without Sally.

Sally and Justin had been killed when a seventeen-year-old boy was distracted by friends in the back seat. He drove through a stop sign at high speed. His car smashed into the driver's door of Sally's Mazda. The impact was so great that Walter was told there was no chance of survival. As with any accident, it was so unnecessary. There was no rational explanation for the death of Sally and Justin.

Walter was trying to get his life back together. He had attended church a few times, but it was too hard to listen to Rev. Wilson's sermons without Sally at his side. After church one Sunday, he decided to organize his workshop. He had barely even entered the room for months.

As Walter sorted through the clutter, he came across his list of unlovable people. That seemed like a long time ago. He had forgotten about his project. At the top of the list was Earnest. He remembered the commotion at Sally's funeral when a filthy homeless man entered the church and sat in the back of the sanctuary. Walter didn't know for sure, but he suspected it was Ernest.

Next on the list was Al Barnes. Walter had heard from Al several times. He worked with Al to finalize the life insurance that was provided by the company, but Al also seemed to be concerned with Walter's well-being. Both of these men understood how it felt to suffer. Walter never tried to locate Sally's cousin Mark. He always thought he would find the same story of a man who was hurt or angry.

Many things had changed during the past six months. Walter realized that his list of unlovable people was no longer accurate. His new list contained only one name - Jason Langley, the young man who had killed his beloved Sally. Because of his immature stupidity, Walter lost everything.

Walter stared at the list, the names blurred by his tears. He realized there was only one name that needed to be there, but he didn't know if he could write it. If Christmas was really about loving the unlovable, he would have to find a way to love Jason.

He thought about it for a long time, late into the afternoon. Walter knew what he had to do. With the same resolve that he had when he started the project, Walter determined that before next Christmas arrived, he would somehow learn to love Jason. Because he knew his own heart, Walter realized that loving the unlovable was God's greatest gift.

What Does God Look Like?

The door to Rick's office had never been slammed in anger before now. The jolt rattled his diplomas hanging on the wall and knocked a book from the shelf. Rick sat in the plush office chair and stared at the door knob. He was numb.

The numbness was not caused by the antagonistic encounter that had just occurred with Martha O'Donnell. He and Martha had been at each other's throats for months, and this was not the first time she had expressed her anger and disgust toward Rick. To be honest, Rick did not really care what Martha did or said.

Rick had been the Pastor at Trinity Church for nearly five years. During his tenure the church had changed from being a one-family-dominated, stagnate congregation to a diverse, energetic fellowship. Although the church showed many signs of health, the changes took an exorbitant toll on Rick.

Martha O'Donnell was known as the church matriarch for nearly three decades, and she was not willing to release her grip without a fight. In her mind, Rick was her primary enemy and if she could get him removed from the pastor's office, she could reassert her power.

At times, the battle between Rick and Martha was intense. They both cared very deeply for the church—they simply disagreed about what was best. They had long since given up the pretense that they were working together, and everyone in the church was aware of the raging conflict between these two worthy opponents.

Rick was tired, and he was numb. The spiritual struggle was more than he was prepared to face. It was obvious that he allowed the clash with Martha to denigrate into personal attacks and unfair tactics. Everyone knew that Rick had even used the Sunday morning pulpit to launch more than one attack.

As Rick tired of staring at the door knob in the wake of Martha's latest tirade, he decided that it was time to give up. If the church truly wanted his leadership, they would have silenced Martha a long time ago. Why should he waste his time on a group of people who did not respect him?

His mind was made up. Rick rose quickly from his chair,

reached for his jacket that was hanging on the coat rack next to the door, and stepped out of the office. His Secretary, Doris, who had sat in stunned silence after Martha slammed the door, turned a compassionate expression toward Rick. Doris understood the conflict better than anyone in the church, but she felt helpless to solve the problem.

"I'll be gone for the rest of the day," Rick said curtly as he hurried out of the office.

He was on his way to announce to his wife that he was resigning from the church. She would not be surprised, but there would be a great deal of apprehension about providing for their family. Becky worked as a bank teller and her salary would not be sufficient to make the house payment and provide for their two young children. Rick knew that Becky would worry, so he would have to reassure her that he could find another job without any trouble.

As he pushed open the door that led to the parking lot, Rick was startled by Adrianne Lockart who was coming into the church. With her usual sanguine excitement, Adrianne squealed when she saw Rick.

"Pastor, I was just coming to see you," she blurted out.

Rick was in no mood to see any church member at the moment, especially someone with Adrianne's enthusiasm.

Not wanting to burden her with his own problems and despair, Rick answered, "You sure seem to be in a hurry, Adrianne. What can I do to help?"

"I need someone to be Joseph for tonight," she said, knowing that Rick would understand. "Walter has the flu and I called Fred, Eric, Donald, and everyone in my Bible study class and everyone else I could think of. Pastor, I don't want you to think you're the last resort, but you're the only one left!"

Adrianne was in charge of Trinity Church's live nativity. Her enthusiasm made this event one of the best programs the church offered. This was the fourth year and it was always so extraordinary that everyone in the community planned to visit the makeshift stable.

Rick had a special place in his heart for Adrianne. She and her husband had come to the church during the first few months after Rick arrived as Pastor. They immediately volunteered to work and were always willing to try anything they were asked. Adrianne had participated in a live nativity in another community and immediately set out to make the one at Trinity the finest in the area. She was successful.

The last thing Rick wanted to do tonight was put on an old bathrobe and stand next to a cow in the freezing cold. Although he planned to keep his intended resignation a secret until after the holidays, he was sure that people would recognize the disinterest on his face.

Sensing Rick's hesitation, Adrianne hastened to add, "It's just for one night. Eric said he could do it tomorrow night!"

"I don't know," said Rick as he tried to think of an excuse. "I was on my way to see Becky, and she might…"

Before he could finish his sentence Adrianne blurted out, "Becky won't mind, she is already planning to bring hot chocolate and coffee. That will work out great. Be here by six so I can make sure the costume fits."

With those final instructions, Adrianne burst out the door, setting off to do something equally important.

Rick wanted to stop her, to shout out that he could not be Joseph, but the words would just not come out of his mouth.

Now what would he do? He did not feel that he could tell Becky about his plans to quit the church. He did not want to ruin the evening for her and the kids. After all, it was Christmas. Even though he felt like Scrooge, that did not give him the right to destroy the holiday.

Not wanting to visit with anyone, he sequestered himself at home. Becky would be at work for several more hours and the kids were still in school. He would be alone with his anger and frustration.

Rick spent the afternoon doing nothing. He glanced through the classifieds in the newspaper to see what jobs were available. After all, he would be looking for a job in the near future. There was nothing of interest, although he tried to convince himself that he could wait tables or deliver pizzas, if necessary, to provide for his family.

The thought of doing something other than pastor a church had never entered Rick's thinking before today. Several of his friends and many seminary classmates were selling insurance or teaching school but Rick had not believed for a moment that such would be his fate.

By the time Becky and the kids came home, Rick was in the kind of mood that would discourage the most experienced optimist. Becky discerned very quickly that Rick was unwilling to talk, so she left him alone. He excused himself from the dinner table and departed early to return to the church, wanting to have more time alone with his anger before the participants in the live nativity arrived.

The familiar route to the church was transformed by Christmas lights and decorations. Rick did not notice the holiday symbols. His thoughts were preoccupied with plans for launching one final attack on Martha O'Donnell. Although he would be leaving the church, he did not want to allow her the opportunity to drag the church back into lethargy.

By the time Adrianne and the others arrived for the nativity preparations, hostility and hatred were oozing out of Rick's heart. It should have been obvious to everyone except they were preoccupied with costumes and hay bales. Rick grabbed his costume and fake beard and dressed quietly in his office. Waiting until the last minute, Rick walked to the front of the church and took his place with Mary and the shepherds, positioned around the manger. He barely spoke more than a simple greeting to the other characters.

Rick was grateful that Adrianne required that no one talk during the live nativity. His goal was to put in the scheduled two hours and go back to the solitude of his office. Although the air was cold and damp, the crowds were large and enthusiastic. The automobile traffic was bumper to bumper at times, and the foot traffic remained at a steady pace. Volunteers distributed Gospel tracts and answered questions posed by visitors. This was the most successful year yet for the live nativity at Trinity Church.

The combination of Rick's anger and the steady pace of the visitors made the evening hours pass quickly. With less than thirty minutes remaining, Rick began to glance at his watch every few minutes, hoping to make the hands move faster. In spite of the fact that he was pretending to be the godly Joseph, he had spent the entire evening planning how to embarrass and humiliate Martha.

Just a few more minutes and everyone could pack up and go home. The traffic had slowed to a normal Friday night pace and there had not been any walking visitors for nearly fifteen minutes. The instant before Rick was ready to tell everyone good night, he noticed two more visitors coming down the sidewalk. He knew it would not take long, so he stayed at his post.

It was a mother and her young son. The boy was excited and dragging his mother, hoping to speed her pace. As they stopped in front of the nativity, the boy stood with an expression of awe on his face. He had never seen such a sight. Especially fascinating were the two sheep and the cow that were grazing next to the shepherds. He began to quiz his mother about the marvelous sights.

"Why are these people standing here with the animals?" he asked his mother.

"That is the nativity," she answered. "It shows the birth of baby Jesus. He was born in a stable and the shepherds came to worship him.

"Why did they worship a baby?" was the boy's puzzled response.

"Because Jesus is the Son of God," explained the mother.

This statement caused the boy to ponder as he continued to examine the unique sight. Finally he asked, "Who is that man standing next to the baby?"

The mother looked toward the manger and said, "That's Jesus' father."

The boy stared into Rick's eyes as if he were searching for more than what was apparent. Finally, in a voice that expressed his confusion, he said, "You mean, that man is God?"

"No, no, that's Joseph" she responded.

"You said that the baby was God's son," replied the boy accusingly.

As is often the case with questions posed by young children, there was not a good answer readily available to the mother. The mother looked at the boy and then she turned her glance to Rick. "That man looks nothing like God!" she said abruptly.

The mother continued to explain the perplexing concept to her son but Rick did not hear anything she said. The words, "That man looks nothing like God!" echoed in his mind.

Rick knew that she was right. For weeks now, he did not look anything like God. Many times Rick had preached that Jesus showed us how God looks in the flesh. He often called upon his congregation to live so that others could see God in their lives. Now, he was the biggest failure.

All night long, hundreds of people had looked at Rick's

portrayal of Joseph. They pictured a loving servant of God who was willing to set aside his own convenience in order to obey God.

It was time to close down the live nativity. Rick was still eager to get back to the privacy of his office. However, now it was not to stir up his anger but to confess his sin and to begin to make things right. For the first time in a long time, he was aware of the power of the baby in the manger.

A Christmas Reunion

The appearance of the first snowflake confirmed Tony's worst fear - it was going to be another cold, wet night. Fresh snow on Christmas Eve is normally a welcome sight. However, for Tony it meant that flagging down a ride from a passing motorist was fraught with new challenges. This was no easy task since anyone driving in this type of weather had to fight the glare of headlights reflecting against the falling snow. It is tough enough just to keep within the boundaries of a traffic lane under these circumstances, much less recognize a pleading hitchhiker.

Tony's mailing address had been "on the road" for several

months, but this was his first Christmas without his family. Even though he was only eighteen years old, Tony was already convinced that the past nine months might have been the most difficult time he would ever experience. At least, that was his hope.

This stretch of highway was usually filled with weary travelers, eager for a companion to help pass the time. On this particular evening, the few vehicles on the road were occupied with excited families, eager to get home before the arrival of Santa. Tony secured a spot alongside the highway that afforded some protection from the wind and began the long wait for a benevolent motorist.

The shelter consisted of a seldom-used railroad trestle that spanned the two-lane highway. It showed promise of being a good location to secure a ride for several reasons. Drivers, unless they were especially daring, needed to maneuver the winding road and narrow bridge at a slower speed, which made a pleading pedestrian more visible. Also, the massive pine beams provided a blockade against the chilling December wind. Tony nudged up against one of the worn bridge supports that offered a shield from three directions. He could still peer down the road far enough to position himself in a more visible location as vehicles approached.

Tony braced himself by pressing his back against the splintered beam. Occasionally, he would bend at the knees and squat like a baseball catcher setting up to receive a pitch to keep his legs from becoming stiff in the cold. Every few minutes it was necessary to brush the large snowflakes from the shoulder of his dark wool coat. He wanted to stay as dry as possible, making him a more attractive potential rider to a passing driver.

The distance between oncoming vehicles lengthened with the passing of each minute. These extended pauses afforded Tony the time to reflect on his distressing situation and the difficult task that awaited him. Although he was attempting to maneuver his way home, he did not foresee a homecoming celebration. He was not sure what kind of greeting a failure should receive, but that is exactly what he anticipated.

Tony's father was a strong, quiet man, the kind who finds it difficult to express any kind of emotion that might be interpreted as soft. He found that he could protect himself from these potential situations by being aloof, not getting involved in the lives of his children. He seldom attended little league games or school plays, but he always asked about them after the fact. Tony was confident that his father cared, but he had never experienced the feeling of being cared for.

If Tony's father was the stereotypical father, then his mother was the stereotypical mother. She gave her life to the children, meticulously attending to every physical need. Her primary goal in life was to keep them clean, well fed, and educated. She was so good at being a mother that it almost seemed routine, rehearsed without feeling.

Tony's family life would have been considered ideal by many young men. His mother and father both cared about him very deeply. They were always quick to forgive and patient with his rebellion. Tony gave them plenty of opportunities to practice both their forgiveness and patience.

Like every teenager, Tony knew his parents did not really understand his thoughts and feelings. How could they comprehend what it was like growing up in his world? He knew they had been teenagers at one time, but times had changed. His world was so different from what they knew.

His Mom and Dad could never give up control. It seems like they questioned everything he did and tried to make him feel guilty for what he did not do. It finally got to be too much. Fighting all the time, demands, rules, it was no fun living at home, so he left.

His first move was to his friend's house, but after about two days, that was no better. Not only did he lose the use of his Dad's car but now he didn't even have his own room. There must be a better place, so Tony set out to find it.

He called his Mom one day and told her that he had a job with a moving company. It was hard work but it would allow him to travel across country. Besides, the pay was pretty good! That was the last time he had spoken with his mother. He did not remember his last conversation with his father, but he knew it was not a pleasant experience.

The moving job seemed like the answer, until they unloaded the van on his very first trip. Not knowing the best way to lift furniture, Tony twisted his back and could not work. He could barely walk and he could certainly not ride in the cab of an eighteen-wheeler. So, they left him behind; all alone in a strange city, five hundred miles away from home.

He managed to find shelter for a few weeks to rest his back. For the next few months he picked up odd jobs whenever possible and became familiar with the community soup kitchens. A homeless bum at the age of eighteen. That was quite an achievement.

On more than one occasion, Tony wanted to pick up the phone and call home. Yet, he had too much pride. He was not ready to admit that he had been wrong. He knew that he would have to make that call someday, but it would take more than a few handouts and homeless nights.

Things began to change at Thanksgiving. Late in October, Tony found a job with a construction crew. It allowed him to rent a very small motel room and get out of the weather at night. One of the foremen took Tony under his wing and extended an invitation for Thanksgiving dinner. He was grateful for the home-cooked meal and the warm, inviting house.

As he ate the Thanksgiving meal, he was reminded of the holidays shared with his own family. Although his Mom was not the best cook in the world, she always prepared a tasty turkey with all the trimmings. He missed his family!

A few days after Thanksgiving, an extended cold spell arrived and shut down the construction business. Once again, Tony was without a job and nowhere to live. He was tired, cold and lonely. He kept remembering his parent's house, but he was afraid he would not be welcome.

Finally, two days before Christmas, Tony knew he had to go home. All of his belongings fit snugly into a large backpack. He strapped it on and began the journey home. He had enough money to buy a few meals along the way, if he could only hitch enough rides to carry him the five hundred miles.

Now, as he watched the snow rapidly increase in intensity, he was less than a hundred miles away, but it was getting very late on Christmas Eve. As Tony anxiously waited for someone to stop and offer him a ride, he pictured his family gathered around the Christmas tree. His Mom and Dad, along with his younger sister, would be singing carols and trying to guess what was in the brightly wrapped presents. His heart began to ache.

Tony was not sure what he would say when he knocked on the front door. He was hoping the words would come to him at the moment. There was much that needed to be said, but he had no idea where to start. He prayed that they would let him come in and stay until he could get on his feet. He would be glad to abide by their rules if he could just get warm and rested.

The snow was starting to cover the ground and Tony could feel the bitter cold on his feet and hands. If someone did not stop soon he would be in real trouble from the weather. In the distance, Tony heard a rattling sound. As the headlights grew brighter, he began to sense that it was an old pickup. The driver spotted Tony hunched over trying to stay warm. He pulled the truck to the side of the road and waited for Tony to walk up to the passenger's window.

The old man was not much for conversation, but he did offer to take Tony to his destination. He was returning from delivering firewood. Tony was grateful for the ride and even more thankful that the old man did not want to talk. He had two hours to sit in silence, resting and contemplating his arrival at home.

As they came to Tony's neighborhood, the sun was beginning to make its morning appearance. Tony thanked his chauffeur and stepped out of the pickup about a block from his parent's house. The snow was still falling, but it did not seem nearly as cold in the morning light and in his old neighborhood.

He picked up his backpack, gathered his courage, and began the walk to the house. The fresh snow covered everything in the yard, but it still looked very familiar. He was the first to make footprints on the sidewalk as he stepped up to the front door. Taking a deep breath, Tony reached out and rang the doorbell.

Even though it was early, Tony knew they would be up, exchanging presents and taking pictures. Christmas day was filled with customs that always seemed silly to Tony until he was too far away to enjoy them. He waited a minute and then pushed the doorbell once again.

He could not hear any sounds from inside, so he knocked loudly on the large wooden door. Finally, he heard the shuffle of feet approaching the door. Tony's nervousness began to increase, as he brushed his hair back in a vain attempt to improve his disheveled looks.

The door slowly opened. Tony could tell that his mother was apprehensive about an uninvited guest this early in the morning. Reassuringly, Tony softly said, "Mom, it's me, Tony."

In one quick move, Tony's mother threw open the door and grabbed him around the neck. Tears began to flow from both of them as they relished the moment they feared would never come. After a few moments of speechless embrace, they realized they were still standing in the cold snow. They hurried into the warm house to continue the reunion.

For the next few hours, Tony and his mother sat at the kitchen table and shared nine months of heartache. When Tony left home, it was only the beginning of family problems. Apparently, his Mom and Dad blamed each other for their failure with Tony. They constantly fought over their wayward son until finally his Dad moved out.

Tony's Mom and younger sister were together in the house, but it would need to be sold soon since they could not make the mortgage payments. His dad was living about forty-five miles away in another city. There had been very little joy for the family this Christmas.

Tony's mother poured the last cup of coffee, and they walked into the family room toward the Christmas tree. His sister was up and even she was glad to see her older brother come home. They sat down next to the tree which had very few presents. There were two or three gifts for Tony's sister and one for his mother.

Just as they prepared to unwrap the gifts, the front doorbell rang. They all looked at one another as if to say, "Who could that be?"

Mom walked to the door as Tony and his sister discussed the anticipated contents of her presents. It was several minutes before there was any sound from the front foyer. Finally, Tony's Mom, holding hands with his Dad, walked into the family room.

Christmas had also reminded Tony's father about what he had lost when he walked away from his family. He spent a very sleepless Christmas Eve, longing to be together as a family. He dressed and drove to his former home, ready to seek his family's forgiveness. What he found exceeded his greatest expectations, as he discovered that his son had also returned.

They were all together once again. There were very few presents under the tree - yet, it was the finest Christmas they would ever experience. Tony's Mom and Dad had received their son as a gift. The gift of a son is the greatest gift ever given at Christmas!

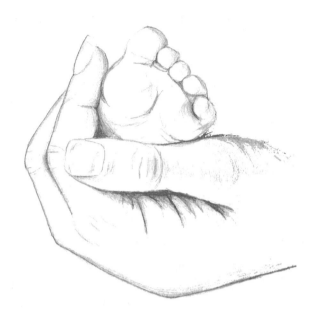

Christmas Hope

As Joe rested on the bed beside his sleeping wife, he finally had an opportunity to catch a breath. He thought to himself, "Christmas Eve is not supposed to be like this!"

He had anticipated a calm celebration, just him and his wife Mary, together in the small house on the edge of town. They had planned to exchange their gifts to one another, perhaps read the Christmas story and share a relaxing time in front of the fireplace.

This was to be the last Christmas for them to be alone as a couple. Mary was pregnant and the baby was due before the end of January. They were already anticipating next

Christmas when they would have a child to share the festivities.

For a twenty-four year old, Joe had already experienced a great deal of life. He was born and raised in a small, northern California town. After high school graduation, Joe did not have many choices to make. The nation was at war with Germany and all the boys became soldiers. Joe was no exception.

He spent a full three years in the army; nearly half of the time was in Europe on the front lines. Joe saw many of his army buddies fall in battle. He was one of the few from his battalion who came home unscathed.

Joe was stationed in France when the war finally came to a close. It took another few months to process the paper work and make the trip back to the states. He could hardly wait to return to his peaceful home town.

Perhaps his greatest anticipation was his beloved Mary. They were high school sweethearts and he knew from her letters that she had remained faithful to him throughout his military days. In spite of the many temptations of the army, Joe had also kept himself for Mary. They both envisioned a lifetime together, filled with happiness and children.

Although he knew that he wanted to settle in the small town where he and Mary were raised, Joe was not sure what he would do for a living. He could always work the farm with his father, but the lifestyle was not appealing to either Joe or Mary. There were not many job opportunities that would provide a decent income for a young family.

The need for a job was solved by Mr. Anderson who owned the local lumber yard. The Andersons had two boys who were close to Joe in age. The three boys had been friends all through school. Mr. Anderson planned for his sons to take over the business when he retired. However, neither of his sons came home from the war.

Not long after Joe returned from the battlefield, Mr. Anderson approached him about working in the lumber yard. His intention was to teach him the business and eventually Joe would take over. The plan suited Joe and seemed to be an answer to prayer.

The lumber yard was a good job and it provided a promising future. Joe and Mary rented a small house on the edge of town and soon discovered that their first child was on the way. Since the baby was expected in January, there were very few presents under the tree. Most of their money was spent on provisions for the new child.

On Christmas Eve, Joe closed the lumber yard early, stopped by the bakery to get some cinnamon rolls for Christmas morning, and went home. He was eager to light the fire and spend a cozy evening at home. It was already cold and the clouds foretold of snow within the next few hours.

Joe walked in the back door, took off his shoes as usual, and stepped into the kitchen. He expected to see Mary at the stove preparing dinner, but she was not in her usual place. He walked through the living room and then called out her name.

A faint cry came from the direction of the bedroom. Joe

walked quickly through the door and saw Mary, lying on the bed, obviously in great discomfort. As he hurried to her side and sat on the edge of the bed, Joe asked, "What's wrong?"

"I have been sick all afternoon," said Mary. "I think the baby is coming! I thought you would never get home."

Joe reached out to take her hand as his mind raced to determine the best course of action. It was too soon for the baby. It was another month until the doctor said it would come.

Quickly, Joe stood up and announced that he would get Doctor Wilson. He ran next door to get help. Mr. McDonald had always been a friendly neighbor and Joe asked if he could go out to the farm and get his mother and father. In the meantime, Mrs. McDonald went to sit with Mary while Joe drove across town to get Doctor Wilson.

The doctor's office was already closed for the holidays, and the note on the front door indicated that he would be out of town for several days. In case of emergency, the note said to call Doctor Goodman in the neighboring town, 30 miles away.

Joe did not know what to do, so he drove back home. Just as he parked in front of the house, his parents arrived with Mr. McDonald. During the short time with Mary, Mrs. McDonald had determined that the baby was indeed about to be born. Joe's mother jumped right in and barked out instructions for the men. It was not unusual for a baby to be born at home but this one was coming much too soon.

Joe waited in the front room with his father and Mr.

McDonald. The entire process only took about twenty minutes but it seemed like three days. The tension was thick and Joe prayed as long and hard as he had ever prayed. Finally, everyone's fears were alleviated when they heard the sound of a newborn baby.

Unable to wait for permission, Joe ran into the bedroom to see his new child. His eyes fell upon Mary. She was in disarray and her face was tired, but there was a glow about her that he had never seen before. In her arms was a tiny baby, a little girl.

The women in the room did not exhibit Joe's enthusiasm. They knew the baby was born too early, and she was very tiny. It had been a difficult birth and they were afraid there might be problems. Mrs. McDonald told Joe that they needed to find a doctor as soon as possible.

Overhearing the request, Mr. McDonald volunteered to make the 30 mile trip to get Doctor Goodman. It would take several hours, so the others made plans to take care of the fragile infant. Joe's father retrieved the crib from the attic and scrubbed it as clean as possible. Mrs. McDonald gingerly held the new baby while Joe's mother helped Mary clean up.

Joe took his place at the foot of the bed, holding Mary's hand while fighting back the tears. He was more frightened than he had ever been while on the front lines in France.

Mr. McDonald finally arrived with Doctor Goodman. The doctor carefully examined the newborn girl and stated that her early arrival probably meant that her lungs were not fully developed. She was having a very difficult time breathing.

The doctor then spoke words that caught everyone's attention. "It is likely that this little girl will not make it through the night. However, if she does, she will have a good chance of survival."

She was too small and fragile to risk a trip to the hospital so all they could do was wait and pray. The crib was placed next to Mary's bed and Joe positioned himself between the new mother and her child. The McDonalds and Joe's parents left the room and Doctor Goodman found a chair in the corner. This would not be a typical Christmas Eve.

Throughout the night the doctor frequently walked over to the crib to check the baby. After several hours, Mary fell asleep from exhaustion. She had lost a significant amount of blood and was very weak herself.

Joe could not sleep. He could hear every sound from the baby and her erratic breaths would not allow him to relax. Occasionally it seemed as if she stopped breathing and Joe's heart would also stop. The anxious night hours provided a lot of time for Joe to think.

He lost track of time but he knew it must be approaching sunrise. Joe stretched out his legs and stood up by the side of the bed. The doctor, who had apparently slipped into a light slumber, was awakened by Joe's movement. He cleared his head and walked over to check the new infant.

Doctor Goodman leaned over the crib and then pressed his ear against the little girl's chest. As he listened to the shallow breathing a smile began to spread across his face.

He straightened up, turned his eyes toward Joe and spoke the words everyone had waited to her.

"Her breathing is much stronger this morning," he whispered. "I think she is going to be all right."

"Are you serious?" stammered Joe.

"Yes," said Doctor Goodman, "I believe this precious little girl is ready to get started with life."

The movement of Joe from the bed had wakened Mary. She listened to the doctor's words. When she heard the good news, tears began to flow down her cheeks.

Joe noticed the joy on his wife's face and he reached down to give her the biggest hug of her life. They were going to be a family!

The folks in the other room heard the commotion and came in to investigate. They saw the excitement and joined the celebration. After a few moments, Mr. McDonald suggested they all pause for a prayer of thanksgiving to God for His gracious answer.

As soon as Mr. McDonald said, "Amen," Joe realized it was Christmas morning. Holding Mary's hand in one hand, and his mother's hand with the other, Joe looked up and said, "Merry Christmas everyone!" It was the start of the greatest Christmas celebration Joe and Mary had ever experienced.

After she finally dried her eyes of all the tears, in a quiet voice, Mary said, "Joe, we need to name our precious little daughter. If you don't mind, I have an idea."

Joe had been so busy that the thought of naming his new

baby girl had not entered his mind.

"Of course you can name her," replied Joe. "What name do you want?"

"I think we should call her Hope," said Mary. "It is Christmas morning and her birth has filled our lives with hope."

The little girl was given the name Hope, because that is what the birth of a baby on Christmas Eve is all about.

A Difficult Decision

People in the Texas Panhandle have worn out the phrase, "There is nothing between us and the North Pole except a barbed wire fence." This was one of those nights when the sentiment would be spoken often.

Even though the north wind was brisk and the air frigid, Jerry was excited about spending the next couple of hours outdoors. For the past three years, he had volunteered to raise money for the Salvation Army during the Christmas season. He spent three or four evenings during the month of December in front of his neighborhood grocery store, ringing a shiny brass bell and smiling at generous shoppers.

Other than the potential for frostbite, there was not much to the job. Jerry liked it because he enjoyed meeting people. He always chose to work from seven to nine in the evening. These hours allowed him to get home, eat dinner with his family, do his civic duty, and still get home in time to watch the evening news. In other words, he could do his part for the community without too much inconvenience.

If you were to ask any of his neighbors or friends, they would all tell you that Jerry is a good man. In fact, that would probably be the exact term they would use. There is nothing outstanding about him, either positive or negative. He is just good. No one wants to be identified as average, but that is an accurate description of Jerry, in both looks and actions.

Jerry and his wife Beth met in college. He was a student because he had nothing better to do, and she enrolled because her father insisted. Neither were in danger of finding their names on the honor roll. After a nine-month romance, they married and began the process of becoming an average family.

Eventually, Jerry was hired by the electric company. At first, he walked neighborhoods reading meters, but eventually he advanced to become a manager. It was a good job, not a great one. It allowed Jerry and Beth to have a fine home and provide the necessities for their two daughters.

Jerry was friendly and well liked, but no one would say that Jerry was their best friend. He always avoided getting too deep into relationships, preferring to reserve time and energy for Beth and the girls. He was a good family man.

Jerry had two reasons for getting charitably involved during the Christmas season. First, he thought it was important to be a contributing member of the community. He didn't want it to ever be said that Jerry Benson ignored his civic duty.

His second reason was more important. Jerry's supervisor at work expected his entire crew to give something to the community during the holidays. It was vital for the image of the electric company, and he required a written report in early January. The few hours Jerry spent in front of the market always paid off during evaluation time at work.

I said there were two reasons that motivated Jerry; perhaps there is a third. Deep in the recesses of Jerry's thoughts was the hope that this simple act of kindness might offset some of the failures in his life when it came time for judgment day. Jerry didn't know much about that, but he was confident God would have to give him some credit for enduring the cold winds of December in the Texas Panhandle. If that is true, this night will prove to be very significant when it comes to Jerry's final appearance before God.

It was already frigid when Jerry arrived home from work. The house was empty and Jerry vaguely remembered that Beth had planned to take the girls shopping after school to finish up their Christmas lists. He found some homemade chili in the refrigerator. At least he would begin the night being warm on the inside. After heating a large bowl of the chili in the microwave, Jerry ate his meal in the company of an old Seinfeld rerun on cable.

After piling his dishes in the sink, Jerry grabbed his

leather gloves and a red Santa hat as he put on a heavy wool peacoat. In ten minutes, he needed to be standing outside the grocery store, clanging the bell to get shoppers' attention.

He found a good place for his car in the store parking lot, underneath a bright spotlight. Normally he didn't worry about someone breaking into his car, but he knew that people were a little more desperate during the Christmas season. While working last week, Jerry noticed some suspicious boys hanging around the parking lot. He felt better about being able to keep an eye on his car from his vantage point in front of the store.

Traffic in and out of the store seemed heavier than normal. Usually on a Friday evening there would not be many shoppers, but since Christmas was just two days away, perhaps they were putting together the ingredients for the holiday meal. More shoppers meant the time went faster for Jerry. There was always someone to greet as they came and went. He also anticipated a good night for the Salvation Army since his bucket was much fuller than usual.

When he had parked his car, Jerry had noticed an older model minivan further out in the parking lot, away from the light. At the time he didn't think much about it, assuming that the owner was in the store. After about fifteen minutes of ringing his bell in front of the store, Jerry noticed a woman with two young children come out of the store. It appeared they went out of their way to avoid eye contact with him. Such an encounter was not that unusual since many people who did not want to make a contribution tried to pretend as if they did not notice him.

Out of the corner of his eye, he watched the woman and the two children walk toward his parked car. They quickly marched past his vehicle and climbed into the minivan parked in the dark. From the way the door opened, it appeared that someone was in the van waiting for them.

Jerry went back to work greeting the holiday shoppers and making inviting gestures to encourage people to drop money into the bucket. After a few minutes, he happened to glance out toward the parking lot and saw a man and another child get out of the minivan and walk toward the store.

The child was a boy, probably about six or seven years old. He wore a lightweight jacket, and what looked like a bath towel wrapped around his shoulders to protect his head and ears from the arctic wind. His hands were buried deep in his jeans pockets and it was apparent he had no gloves.

The man was dressed in equally light, almost summer clothing. A Houston Astros baseball jacket offered little protection against the panhandle cold. His hair was disheveled and his face, unshaven for several days. The man's eyes had the tired look of someone who had not slept well for a long time. Like the woman before him, he went out of his way to avoid an encounter with Jerry and his ringing bell.

The next thirty minutes went by quickly for Jerry. It was approaching eight o'clock and business at the grocery store was tapering off rapidly. Although he had only been about the task for an hour, the cold weather and the fast pace of the holiday season were beginning to take a toll. He was tired and looked forward to the final hour of his holiday service to the community.

The man from the minivan, tightly gripping the young boy's hand, came out of the store. They walked slowly toward their vehicle in the dark corner of the parking lot. It was obvious that he did not make any purchases, which caused Jerry to wonder if he was observing some kind of elaborate theft.

Jerry expected the see the minivan drive off, but it did not move. Instead, after a few minutes, the side door slid open and the woman and the two young girls stepped out into the night air. The tired woman pulled a scarf around her ears as she picked up the smallest of the girls. The other girl almost had to run in order to keep up with the woman's rapid gait toward the store. Once again they walked past Jerry without a hint of his presence.

Jerry observed this strange procession in and out of the store until it was time for him to shut down his work for the evening. He gathered the money into the bank bag and took it in to the store manager according to the prearranged process for handling the donations. Pulling his jacket up around his ears, Jerry stepped out of the store and began to trot toward his car. He hoped that Sarah and the girls had not finished off the chili because another bowl would be warm and refreshing when he got home.

As he started to unlock his car, Jerry was close enough to notice more details about the minivan. The engine was not running and he could tell that frost had built up and coated the inside of the windows. Vague shadows were moving inside and he thought he could hear a child's cry.

He didn't know what was going on but felt like he needed to do something. Reluctantly, Jerry walked up to the driver's door and tapped on the window. He waited for a few seconds but there was no response from inside. He rapped on the window once again. This time the window slowly opened about halfway.

With a slight stutter in his voice, Jerry said, "I couldn't help but notice you folks out here all evening. Is there something I can do to help you?"

The man bowed his head as if he were studying something on the steering wheel. Then he turned to his right and whispered something to the woman in the passenger's seat. He swung back toward Jerry and began to roll up the window. Once the window was closed, the door slowly opened and the man stepped out into the cold air.

Jerry could hear one of the children ask, "Where's Daddy going?"

Without looking at Jerry, the man said, "I'm sorry; we don't mean to be a problem. We'll move on!"

"I didn't mean that you are a problem," replied Jerry, "I just wanted to know if I could help with something."

A relieved look spread across the man's face as he looked up at Jerry.

For the next four or five minutes the man related his story. It was as if he was hoping for someone to listen.

The man, his wife, and three young children were from Houston. He had been without work for several months. Despite his most diligent efforts, there were no jobs to be found. All of their resources were exhausted; they even lost their house.

A friend told them that if they could make it to Seattle that he would help him find a job. They sold everything they had, packed their personal belongings in the van, and headed north. Just outside of town, the transmission failed and it took their final dime to get the vehicle running.

Here they were. Hundreds of miles from any family, several days short of their destination, and no money. They did not even have money to run the engine so they could stay warm. The trips in and out of the store allowed them to take turns getting warm. They knew it was not a long-term solution, but at this point, they were just hoping to make it through the night.

A few minutes earlier, Jerry thought he was finished with the task of helping the poor - now he wasn't so sure. Initially, he thought about the forty dollars in his wallet. That would allow them to buy a tank of gas and a warm meal. But, he knew that was not much under these circumstances.

He began to create a mental list of all the local community organizations. He had lived in this town for a long time, and he knew there were folks who would help. It was late on Friday evening and it might be hard to find someone, but that would certainly be the least he could do.

However, for some reason, even that seemed like an insufficient response. He knew what needed to happen, but he also had numerous reasons why he should just leave it alone. He knew they had plenty of room in their house and there was more than enough food in the freezer. It might be a tough sell, but Jerry was confident that Sarah would be agreeable.

But, how could he invite complete strangers to stay in his house. He didn't know anything about these folks. It is possible that the whole story was made up. Maybe they were just looking for an easy target who would fall for their sob story. How could he put his family at risk?

As he stood there and thought about what to do, Jerry was freezing. He knew the man and his family were even colder, so a decision had to be made. What would he do?

Jerry quickly made up his mind and told the concerned father to get back in his van. "Follow me," he said, as he made his way to his own vehicle. Jerry escorted the frozen van to the service station that sat on the corner lot. Motioning for the man to pull up to the pumps, Jerry got out and began to fill the van with gas. He used his credit card to pay for the gas and then once again shouted to the family, "Follow me!" as he climbed back into his own car.

The confused family must have thought Jerry was some kind of mad man but they didn't have any better options, so they followed. Jerry led them on the short five-minute drive to his house where he motioned for them to pull into the driveway.

Jerry scurried over to the passenger's side of the van and helped bundle up the kids to keep them warm until they got inside the house. He nearly had to wrestle the mother and father to get them to accept his invitation, but they were too cold and desperate to put up a significant fight.

As he pushed open the door and escorted his new friends into the warmth of his house, Jerry was not sure of the exact words he would speak to Sarah and the girls, but he was confident that he was doing the right thing.

After all those years of helping raise money for the nameless, faceless poor in the community, Jerry finally met them in person. This year's report about his community service during the holidays would be significantly different.

A Cry in the Dark

After fourteen years on the Police force, Joe Morgan thought he should at least have the night off on Christmas Eve. However, that was not the case, so he found himself walking the familiar streets of his precinct.

Christmas Eve was never busy for a policeman. All the stores in his neighborhood closed by five, six at the latest. Once the shoppers were finished, everyone hurried home to be with family and friends, and the only people on the streets were the few procrastinators.

Joe's shift did not end until midnight, so he anticipated a long evening at the station, joking and laughing with the other officers who had the misfortune of working on Christmas Eve. He really didn't mind because he would get home in time to get a good night's rest before the family celebration on Christmas Day.

It was nearly six o'clock and Joe had already made the rounds of the entire neighborhood once. The only shop remaining open was the variety store owned by Mac Williams. Mac was a hard worker and he wanted to make sure not to miss even one customer, so he stayed open a little later than everyone else.

Mac did not keep his shop open out of greed; his motivation was necessity. With the help and support of his wife Betty, Mac had opened the store as a very young man. He had been a successful businessman, and Betty was very frugal with their money. Everything was set to allow them to sell the business and retire comfortably.

Plans, especially long-range plans, are not always realized. Mac and Betty had a son who would have been forty-two this Christmas, if he had lived. John was Mac's pride and joy. He did well in school and was a good athlete in high school. Mac spent many evenings in the winter and spring watching his son excel on the basketball court.

A loving, supportive wife, a talented over-achieving son, and a successful business-life was good for Mac.

John was offered a scholarship to play basketball for a small college in the south. Mac was hesitant to let him go, primarily because he would not get to see his son play. As you would expect with an eighteen-year-old, John insisted and finally Mac gave his blessing.

In college, John quickly discovered that his athletic skill had reached its limit and he could not compete. His disappointment led him into other activities, many of them unhealthy. He slowly fell into the grip of alcohol and then drugs.

Mac did everything he knew to do. He gave him money, he pleaded, he screamed, he paid for treatment, but nothing worked for any length of time. All Mac could see was the tremendous potential of his son, so he refused to give up hope.

John fought his addiction for more than fifteen years until it finally took his life. Mac did everything humanly possible; in fact, in hindsight it is easy to say that he tried to do too much. Legal fees, medical bills, and funeral expenses consumed everything that Mac and Betty had accumulated.

Not only did Mac lose his son and his life's savings; his relationship with Betty was forever changed. They stayed together but they were both filled with anger. Betty was angry with John for ruining their family and Mac was angry about everything.

There was nothing at home any longer, so Mac gave himself completely to the shop. There was no hope of retiring. It took all his effort just to be able to take care of their basic needs.

Joe was not surprised to discover that Mac's shop was the only one still open late on Christmas Eve. When he leaned inside the shop door to wish Mac a Merry Christmas, all he received in return was a gruff growl.

As he stepped away from the shop to continue surveying the neighborhood, Joe thought he heard a noise from the alley on the north side of the building. As he walked into the dark corridor, he was startled by a yellow cat that jumped out of the shadows. Assuming that the feline was the cause of the noise he heard, Joe continued down the street, checking locked doors while humming Christmas carols.

He would later regret that he did not inspect the alley more thoroughly. The noise was caused by a rugged looking young man who appeared to have slept in his clothes for more than a week. The vagrant saw Officer Morgan and ducked behind a trash can hidden in the dark shadows of the alley.

When the police officer turned and walked away, the young man jumped to his feet and continued his path toward the entrance to the alley. He had had his eye on Mac's store all evening as he waited for the right time to make his move.

Appearances were correct; he had slept in his clothes for several days-enough that he had lost count. Brad was a stranger to the city. After years of conflict with his father finally boiled over, Brad left home to find his fame and fortune, or at least some freedom.

His girlfriend Lisa soon followed, to be with her lover and the father of her expectant child. Neither of their parents knew about the pregnancy or about the fact that their children were sleeping on the street.

Brad and Lisa did not know when the baby was due, but

they knew it would be soon. Lisa had not been to a doctor. When you don't have money for rent, you certainly don't have money for a doctor. Although they were both lonely and afraid, they were also too proud to return home.

Sleeping in alleys and under bridges meant long, cold nights. Brad noticed that Mac's store had a display of jackets and blankets near the front door. They were just what he and Lisa needed to make it through another night.

Tiptoeing to the edge of the brightly lit store, he looked both ways, not only to make sure the policeman was gone, but also to be certain that no one else was coming. The street was very quiet and there was no one close enough to see. He could tell that Mac was getting ready to close the store, so his action would have to be quick and decisive.

The young man came out from the shadows, took four running steps to the front of the store and darted inside. The storeowner had his back turned, so he was confident of a clean escape.

His eyes quickly scanned the jackets and blankets. He picked out two of each. He chose them because they seemed to be the heaviest, and he wanted as much warmth as possible.

Clutching the merchandise next to his chest, the young man quickly moved out the front door. Just as he stepped on the threshold, he heard Mac's voice, "Hey, you! Stop!"

Brad hesitated for just an instant and then made a quick dash out the door toward the alley. He knew he could outrun the old man and hide in the dark shadows of the alley.

Mac reached under the counter, grabbed a pistol that he

kept for just such an occasion and ran in hot pursuit. He was surprised at how quickly he could still move. His body was filled with adrenaline and anger.

As he bolted through the front door, Mac saw the young thief turn down the alley. Recklessly, he aimed the gun in the general direction and fired two quick shots. He knew it was unlikely that he would hit a moving target but maybe it would cause the thief to slow down.

By now, Officer Joe Morgan was on the other side of the block. When he heard the unmistakable sound of gunfire, his heart raced. He suspected that it involved Mac, because he was the only person he had seen for quite some time. Joe decided to cut through the alley, which would be the quickest path to Mac's shop.

When the two bullets flew past Brad's ear, he stumbled and fell into a pile of empty boxes lining the alley. By the time he regained his feet, Mac was close behind. Brad tried to find the darkest shadows, so he could hide, but he realized that he had been caught.

Mac was about twenty feet behind him, screaming and cursing. Another shot was fired and Brad was no longer afraid of being caught. He was afraid of dying.

Just as Brad stopped to surrender and plead for mercy, Officer Morgan appeared from the other end of the alley. His pistol was drawn in anticipation of responding to the gunfire. When Joe realized that it was Mac, he breathed a quick sigh of relief.

However, before he could catch a second breath, Joe Morgan discovered that he was in the wrong place. His sprint had placed him right in the line of fire. He stood directly between Mac and the captured thief.

Mac, holding the gun with both hands, had it aimed at the culprit's head, which meant that it was aimed directly at Joe. Mac was cursing and screaming about being robbed for the last time, and it was obvious from the look in his eyes that he planned to finish the job.

This was one of the moments a police officer trains for, but hopes never comes. Joe quickly pointed his revolver toward the shooter and demanded with his most authoritative voice that Mac put the gun on the ground.

All of the anger and frustration that had built up in Mac over the years was about to explode. He was determined to kill the thief, even if it meant losing his own life. He was tired of having what he had worked for taken away from him; he was tired of living.

At that moment, Betty came running around the corner and into the alley. She saw her husband and a police officer standing face to face, pointing guns at one another. Her voice joined the screaming, as she began to plead for Mac to stop.

In spite of the finest police training available and fourteen years of experience, Joe was at a loss. He knew that he had only a few seconds to make a decision, because he could see the anger and determination in Mac's eyes. His training told him to take the first shot, but his heart would not allow his hand to squeeze the trigger. He also knew that if he dove out of the way, Mac would kill the young man. Even though he did not know Brad, Joe knew that his job was to protect him.

In the midst of the confusion and confrontation, everyone heard the unmistakable cry of a woman in pain. The cry of pain was followed by a soft call for help. They all stopped for just a moment and then they heard it again, "Please help me!"

Mac lowered his gun and Joe breathed a sigh of relief. Brad, who had almost died already from fear for his life seemed to know the source of the plea. He turned and walked carefully toward a pile of old blankets and newspapers tucked away in the shadows.

"Lisa, I'm right here," he said.

"Brad," she said, "It's time for the baby. We've gotta get some help!"

By this time Joe, Mac, and Betty all approached near enough to see the young girl about to give birth.

Betty was the first to spring into action. She began to bark out orders to everyone.

"Call for an ambulance!" she hollered in Joe's direction.

"Mac, go get some warm blankets!"

"Young man, if you are with this girl, get over there and hold her hand!"

Everyone responded according to instructions and within a few minutes the emergency medical crew arrived.

In all the excitement over the needs of this soon-to-be-mother, Mac forgot about the young man stealing his merchandise. Officer Morgan remembered the gunshots, and it would take awhile to calm down from looking down the barrel of a revolver. However, on this night, Christmas Eve, he was not going to say anything to Mac. His lecture could wait for another day.

By the time the ambulance crew had Lisa ready to be transported to the hospital, Mac and Betty had listened to Brad's story. They were saddened, and it seemed like they still had room in their hearts to love. In fact, Betty rode in the ambulance and Mac followed along in his car to the hospital.

Everyone was gone. All the shops were dark and the streets were empty. Joe sat on the curb, alone with his thoughts of what had just happened. He realized how close he came to losing his life or killing another man. He did not know which would have been worse. How many lives would have been destroyed if it were not for the cry of a young woman about to give birth?

At that moment it became obvious to Joe that this Christmas Eve was a lot like the first Christmas Eve. The painful cry of a woman in labor and the faint sound of a newborn infant and suddenly everything is different.

A Very Cold Christmas

The cold snow that covered the walk leading up to William's isolated cabin was no match for the frigid feel in his heart. On the outside, the snow provided a beautiful covering for the New Mexico landscape. On the inside, the cold was devastating.

Just a few years ago, William dreamed about spending the winter in the Rocky Mountains. A day spent on skis, an evening with self-indulgent friends, and a night of uninhibited passion was his idea of paradise. Although he finally made it to the mountains in the winter, there were no skis, friends, or passion. William admitted that he no longer knew what paradise was like, but he knew this was not it.

William slowly lifted his head from the flat pillow. He rolled to his side and supported himself with his elbow. He could see that the sun was shining but he had no idea what time it was. It didn't matter anyway. It had been at least three days, perhaps four, since he had had any contact with another human. His desire was to be alone and for the first time in his life, he actually got what he wanted.

His blank stare was interrupted by a loud crack from the fireplace. The remaining embers from the only source of heat in the room were almost exhausted. William summoned what was left of his depleted energy and rose out of bed. His feet shuffled on the cold wooden floor as he went to arrange a few more logs before the spark was totally lost.

Every effort that was made toward survival stirred an internal debate within William. "Why bother?" he thought to himself, "Why should I expend the little energy I have left on making myself comfortable!" As far as he was concerned, he would be dead in a few more days. It would probably take weeks before anyone who knew him would be notified.

The dry logs quickly ignited from the smoldering ashes. As the flames grew, the fresh warmth began to swallow up the cold of the room. However, the heat did nothing to thaw out the chill of William's soul. He slowly crawled back into bed and sought comfort from his familiar thoughts of despair.

Being cold always took William back to his childhood. Not because of arctic blasts, since he grew up in Mississippi, but because of the emotional isolation and chill that he experienced growing up. If you were William's biographer, you would probably say he was a child of privilege. His parents were among the country club set of the Deep South. Because his father worked, a lawyer by profession, there was never any fear of financial deprivation.

His mother also worked. She was a socialite. Her job did not generate any direct income, but it did contribute to the family status in the community. William's parents were a great partnership and they were very successful at their chosen occupations. Parenting was not their chosen profession.

William was looked upon as a social inconvenience or an occupational hazard, depending on the mood of the moment. All of his physical needs were provided more than adequately by the best caregivers money could buy. Depending upon the employee at the moment, even some of his emotional needs were served by some of the better caretakers.

A studied psychologist would probably tell you that William became an overachiever in order to gain acceptance and approval. That would be a fair assessment that even William would not disagree with. As far back as he could remember he tried everything he could just to be held, hugged, and approved by either Mom or Dad. It never happened!

Although he did not achieve his primary goal, by the time he finished high school, William possessed an incredible array of talent and ability. He could have chosen academics or athletics as his ticket to success. Instead, he chose music. Not classical or popular, but hard and heavy rock. As an eighteen year-old, William saw his music as the best way to express himself.

An amazing thing happened. His music, which he wrote and performed out of his feelings of rejection, actually brought him acceptance and affirmation. Not by his parents, he had already given up on them-but by the music world. He had two songs that climbed to the top of the charts, and William was a star.

The story of the next few years of his life has already been written by hundreds of other rock stars. Drugs, sex, and rock-n-roll is more than the cry of anguished youth; it was the biography of William.

You might expect that William woke up in a gutter one morning as a broken down bum. However, that never happened. He came to his senses before he exhausted his money and talent. Through a series of unusual circumstances, he met a girl named Susan. They were an unlikely pair but they became close friends.

Susan was also a singer, but her stage was the church choir. William was amazed that Susan was not ashamed to be seen with him, so he would occasionally go to church to listen to her sing. She had a good voice but what really caught his attention were the friendships she enjoyed. Everyone loved Susan just as William had always wanted to be loved.

Giving up his lifestyle was easier than you might expect.

He cut his hair, changed his wardrobe, cleaned up his language, and joined the church choir. His musical talent was quickly noted and before long, he was assigned the solo parts. It was impossible to miss the amazing transformation that had taken place in William's life.

When the pastor asked William to share his experience with the church, William discovered another talent. The congregation was mesmerized by his words. It was a story that was worth telling over and over. Soon, William was on the circuit. He and Susan would sing and then he would relate his experience of transformation.

It appeared that William finally had the love and acceptance he had sought since childhood. He was invited to address large congregations and overflowing conventions. Everyone wanted to hear his story and it got a little bit better each time he told it. He was being embraced with the loving arms of the church.

Susan was the first to recognize that there had not been a real transformation. Sure, he had cleaned up his act and played for a different audience, but she knew that William was still the same man she had met years before. She denied it for a long time, hoping her intuition was wrong, but there was finally too much evidence to ignore.

When Susan began to withdraw her affection, William sought comfort in the arms of other women. Although they were not as accessible as in the world of rock and roll, there were always people who wanted to be near the fame and limelight. Susan allowed William to keep up the pretenses for nearly a year. However, the rumors of his infidelity were soon too rampant to ignore. He was cast aside by the church as just another flash in the pan. He had to be pushed away to make room for the next rising star.

The logs in the fireplace had produced a roaring fire. With the swipe of his foot, William cast the blanket onto the floor. Although he was feeling the pangs of hunger, he had no desire to get off the bed and find something to eat. Besides, there wasn't anything in the cabin worth eating. He was somewhat amazed that his despair would even allow him to think about eating a meal.

He had come to this place in order to vanish. He had searched for the most isolated location he could find. The cabin belonged to a monastery. It was offered to seekers who needed to be alone in their search for God. How ironic. William had already found God and His people. Now his goal was to lose himself. He did not have the courage to take his own life with violence, but he did plan to just walk off into the snow-covered mountainside and disappear. It would be several days before he was even missed and might be spring before his body would be found.

If he was going to end it all, now was the time! William stood to his feet to survey the cabin one final time. A leather bag with a few clothes, a toothbrush, hairbrush, and a framed picture of Susan was all that he had. His driver's license was in his pocket so when they found his body they could easily identify him. He was confident that his life would be over before tomorrow's sunrise.

There was a noise outside the door of the cabin. It sounded like feet shuffling in the snow. As William strained to listen, there was suddenly three quick taps on the wooden door.

"Hello! Is anyone there?" inquired the masculine voice from outside.

"Who could that be?" thought William. He had not seen anybody for days. How could anyone know that he was here?

Curiosity won out and William walked over and slowly opened the door. The bright sun glistening off the white snow temporarily blinded him. As his eyes adjusted, he made out the figure of a man wearing a heavy wool coat and a knit cap.

"Merry Christmas!" said the man as William appeared in the doorway. "I brought you some Christmas cheer. I have hot soup and some fruit." He stretched out his hands containing a thermos and a canvas bag filled with oranges.

"Who are you?" William asked uncomfortably.

"I'm Brother Michael," was the cheerful reply. "I'm from St. Bartholomew's," as he pointed in the direction of the monastery. "I didn't know if you were still in the cabin or not but I didn't want you to feel alone on Christmas day."

"I was just leaving," said William, "I didn't realize that it was Christmas."

"You have been isolated! I hate to tell you this but you are not going anywhere for a few days. The snow has closed all the roads and because of the holiday it will probably be several days before highway crews make it up this far.

William didn't know what to say but that didn't matter, Brother Michael took charge of the conversation. "Mind if I come in and share some of this soup with you? It's really cold out here and I would like to thaw out before I return to the main building."

Before William could object, Brother Michael pushed his way into the cabin and was digging through the cabinets for two clean bowls. As he realized what was happening, William began to worry about his appearance. His hair was disheveled, his face had not felt a razor in nearly a week, and his clothes definitely had the slept in look.

It did not seem to matter to Brother Michael. As they sat at the table eating the soup, he deftly guided the conversation from the subject of cold snow to the condition of William's soul. After more than an hour, William was amazed that he had shared his pain and anguish with a complete stranger. Even more amazing was that Brother Michael did not condemn him for his mistakes nor scold him for his despair.

By the time they finished off a second bowl of soup, it was as if William and Brother Michael had been lifelong friends. William had never felt more comfortable with another human being. For the first time in his life he felt accepted, not because of his accomplishments but just because he was William.

It was not difficult to convince William to leave the lonely cabin and join the others at the main campus. He gathered up his few possessions, wrapped himself in a blanket, and walked out the door with Brother Michael. It was hard to believe that a few hours earlier he had planned to walk through that same door and lose himself in a blanket of snow.

Just a few feet from the front of the cabin, William stopped. Brother Michael turned and asked, "Did we forget something?"

Fighting back the tears, William said, "No, I was just thinking about the great gift you gave to me."

"It was good soup, but you have probably had better," replied Michael.

"No, I don't mean the soup," William said, "I mean the gift of life!"

As they turned to walk away from the cabin, Michael put his arm around William. The warmth of the embrace was nothing compared to the new warmth in William's heart.

Killed On a Friday Morning

Ron died early on a Friday morning. He was deep in a Vietnamese jungle, thick with insects; some biting, most harmless, all were bothersome. But the insects didn't kill him.

The heat on that day was stifling. Perhaps it was stagnant air caused by some type of high pressure weather system that parked overhead, but more likely it was the residue of excessive gunfire, exploding ordinance, and burning napalm. Neither the heat nor the ammunition caused his death.

Ron's platoon was ordered to this location to secure a

village that was responsible for the regrettable deaths of several American soldiers. Ron approached every mission with the eagerness of a soldier who had volunteered for this war in order to serve his country. It was an attitude that was not often shared by his bunkmates. He spent many nights defending the rightness of this war to anyone who would be foolish enough to raise the subject. He was as intent on winning the entire war as he was on winning every battle that he fought in the God-forsaken jungle.

Most soldiers couldn't understand why they were fighting for this piece of useless earth, nor could they comprehend why anyone else would be willing to die to take it away from them. It was a war that made no sense, fought by soldiers who were asked to do senseless things. Something had gone horribly awry with the human condition.

The platoon of only eighteen young Americans, too immature by most standards to be called soldiers, was all that was left of the original fifty-five. The eldest, at age twenty-one, had been made sergeant simply because he was the oldest one standing. He was responsible for marshaling these boys who still had the indentions caused by their high school graduation mortarboards on their foreheads.

Always toward the front, as close to the sergeant as possible was Ron. He wanted to fire the initial shot and the final winning blast of every battle. His thirst for combat made Sylvester Stallone look cowardly. He was on a quest to kill as many commies as possible and prove that his country was supreme.

On this particular Friday morning, Ron was among the first quartet of soldiers to enter the village. They took no comfort in the quiet that filled the air because silence often preceded intense battle. They were cautious, but confident that their comrades coming from the other side of the village would provide any protection they needed. Such was the case on this Friday morning. There were no enemy threats to anyone in Ron's platoon as they entered the village.

Even though there was no gunfire, no explosions, and no hostile activities of any kind, Ron still died. It would be inaccurate to say that he was killed in action because really, he was killed in inaction. It was something he saw; something he experienced that killed Ron.

The Army did not award him a medal of honor or even a purple heart. They just shipped him home.

Once back on American soil, Ron's family was expected to take care of all the details and plans. The only things that Uncle Sam provided were a few papers describing meager benefits that might be available under the right circumstances.

Other than the normal wear and tear you would expect from spending ten months in an Asian jungle, Ron's body bore no signs of having been in combat. In fact, just by looking at him, you would not believe that he lived in constant peril, walking the thin tightrope that kept him from falling into death. Ron died on a Friday morning, but he did not arrive back in the States for another four months.

There is more than one way to die. When I say that Ron died, I don't mean that his body ceased to function. In fact, his body didn't die at all; it was not even injured. Something happened on that sweltering morning deep in the Vietnamese jungle that killed Ron on the inside. He was not the same man.

Something he saw in that village was guilty of his murder. If I knew what it was I would certainly tell you. I would like to know myself. I can only imagine. You've seen the pictures of that horrible war - the naked little girl running through the streets with scorched skin, or the soldier shot in the head while on his knees praying to whatever god he claimed as his deity. These were only some of the hideous experiences of that war, perhaps not even the worst. What Ron saw on that Friday morning must have equaled or surpassed them in horror. No one knows.

Ron could never bring himself to discuss his experience. Whatever he saw on that unforgettable hour in a distant swamp would remain vaulted in his mind. It was the kind of memory that causes a man to pray for amnesia or dementia. Among the others in his platoon, only a handful survived long enough to return home. They have nothing to say either, although none of them appear to have been affected like Ron. Perhaps it was because he was such a gung-ho combatant that it was a massive shock to his system. Whatever it was, it killed Ron on that Friday morning.

Waking up alone was nothing unusual for Ron. Even though he had no reason to expect differently this morning, his right arm stretched hopefully across the bed, feeling for the warmth of another body. He found nothing. He was still alone.

Pulling the flannel blanket up underneath his chin, Ron sought relief from the early morning chill that had filled his small room. He always slept better when the house was cold, but it stifled incentive for getting up in the morning. The combination of the temperature and loneliness made it almost pointless to leave the bed. Even when he did get up, there was very little for Ron to do that could be labeled as worthwhile.

But, get up he did. Just like every other morning. He sat on the side of the bed for a few moments, not so much to get his bearings but to contemplate his life. He caught himself doing that a lot in the past few weeks. Ron had always been introspective, even as a kid, but now the inward drift of his thoughts seemed to be out of control at times.

No new revelations this morning, so Ron rose to his feet and walked across the room to make some coffee.

Ron lived in a very basic two-room cabin. One room was the bathroom. The other room was everything else. He did not own a coffee maker; he still used an old-fashioned percolator-the kind that sits on a burner and boils the water until it turns into coffee. He had been making and drinking his coffee like this for so long that the process required no thought. Unless you are accustomed to sipping coffee strong enough to scour grease off a driveway, you would not want to sample Ron's mixture. But, his black juice was more than sufficient to feed his addiction.

The most notable feature of Ron's cabin was the stacks of books that populated the room like prominent columns in a Roman public building. It seemed that every corner of the roof was supported by a chimney of paper, both hardback and paperback. Since he spent little time and energy relating to live human beings, Ron had never-ending hours to fill. He did so by reading. His taste was for nothing in particular and everything in general-novels, current events, history, classics. If he could find a promising book as he surveyed the shelves of local used-book-stores, it would eventually make its way to his pile of books to read and ultimately moved to his pile of books already read.

The wooden cabin, about the size of a two-car garage, was located in the Colorado Mountains, just a few miles beyond the city limits on highway ninety-one running north out of Leadville, a mining town that had realized its glory days a century ago. He had settled into this cabin more than three years previously when he had been looking for a place to nurture his loneliness.

Ron returned home from Vietnam early in 1972. It was obvious that he would not simply slip back into his old way of life. The war had changed him in ways that were not good. The gregarious, enthusiastic young man who had actually volunteered to join the army came back as a quiet, surly man who found it impossible to develop long-term relationships.

He tried to discover his old self. He made frequent visits to the military psychiatrist assigned to his case, he talked with the family pastor several times, he tried drugs and alcohol, but nothing helped. The Ron that he remembered from the past, the one known to his family and friends, was killed on a Friday morning in the clammy jungle.

The only thing he really wanted was to be alone as much as possible. That's why he found his diminutive mountain cabin and settled in.

Choosing a lifestyle of aloneness is not difficult to finance so Ron spent the summers working for an adventure company, leading small groups of tourists on daylong raft rides. Living in the Colorado mountains allowed him to blend in with the hippies and other Vietnam War cripples, so no one expected much from him. That is exactly what Ron wanted, so he was as happy as possible for a man in his condition, although happy is not a word you would ever associate with Ron.

Ron generated enough income during the busy summer months, guiding awestruck tourists through the tricky rapids that he had little need for working once the weather turned frigid. If he ever needed a little extra spending cash during the winter months, nearby ski resorts were always searching for willing hands. He could work as much or as little as he wanted. The determining factor was the amount of income he needed to maintain his austere lifestyle. Consequently, he worked very little during the winter-shortened days.

This year, his finances held strong until very late. In fact, it was nearly Christmas before it was necessary to maneuver his pickup across the twenty-five miles of winding mountain highway to the nearest ski resort. They knew Ron and they knew he could be counted on to do what he was asked. They also knew not to bother with any small talk since it was obvious that he was not interested.

On the Saturday that proved significant in Ron's life, he

traversed to the ski resort early in the morning to get in a full day on the time clock. Since he had to drive across snow packed roads, he might as well get as much overtime pay as possible, so he stayed at the job until the entire work force was sent home for the night. He anticipated a healthy check come payday.

To say the ski resort was busy would be stating the obvious. It was Saturday and it was Christmas Eve. All the factors were precisely aligned to create a profitable day with extensive lift lines and hoards of excited enthusiasts. Most people, Ron included, did not pay attention to the massive amount of snow that fell throughout the day. After all, when your intention is to enjoy the snow, there really cannot be too much.

By the time a weary Ron climbed into his heavily worn Ford to return home, the highway toward his cabin was crammed with snow. The highway department workers struggled to keep the flaky powder pushed to the sides in order to create a passable surface, but with the torrential fall, it was a losing battle. Fortunately, Ron was intimate with the winding road, so it did not matter that he drove blind except for a few feet in front of his pale headlights.

The fifteen or so miles down Highway Twenty-Four were passable, as long as Ron kept his vehicle moving at less than twenty miles per hour. Having crested a hill, Ron allowed himself to exceed that amount on one occasion and the rear end of his pickup began to lose traction. It is an unmistakable, rapidly recognizable feel for a veteran mountain driver. Quickly, Ron lifted his tired leg just enough to remove his right foot from the muddy gas peddle. Simultaneously, he acted against natural instinct and instantly moved his left hand to join with his right in grasping the vinyl covered steering wheel to aim the front tires in the same direction as the slide. Although it seemed longer, it only took a second of time to right the direction of the Ford and regain complete control. He would watch his speed more carefully from now on.

The trip into and through Leadville transpired without further incident, but Ron still had a few miles to go, north on Highway Ninety-One. Being a less-traveled road, there was more snow and it was obvious that it did not benefit from as many passes by the snow plow. The going was much slower, but Ron was determined to make it home. Even though he would be alone, he did not want to spend Christmas Eve in any bed but his own.

The trip from the town limits to his house usually only took eight to ten minutes, but on this night Ron had already estimated that the last lights of Leadville faded from his rear view mirror a half hour ago. There was no one else on the road since Ron saw neither the golden glow of head lights nor the crimson radiance of tail lights along Highway ninety-one.

It was impossible to see any of the familiar landmarks that normally guided travelers, but Ron was confident that he knew where to turn to make the three-quarter mile drive to his cabin. However, he miscalculated. As Ron swerved to the left to aim toward home, the tired pickup plunged like a drunken man down a four-foot embankment, landing nose first onto a massive stone covered with new snow. Somehow, Ron avoided whacking his head on the windshield although he did twist his back trying to brace himself.

The engine roared, for a few seconds, like the start of a NASCAR event, and then came to a sudden halt. Shaking his head to clear his thoughts, Ron was immediately conscious of the total silence that is common during a mountain snowstorm. Other than the soreness in his back, Ron did not detect any other injuries. He had hope. Since he was uninjured, he was confident that the short distance to his cabin would be no problem on foot. It would only be a matter of minutes until he would be wrapped in a warm blanket, anticipating a cup of his own special coffee.

He tugged the lever on the inside of the driver's door and pushed it open with his left arm like he had done so many times before. The pickup was resting at a thirty-five degree angle, so the door almost flew out of his hand from the yank of gravity. Ron cautiously swiveled to his left and steadied himself to step out of the truck. With his left foot, he felt for something solid to sustain his weight. As he pushed his foot through several inches of snow, he tapped his toe on a firm rock that he could trust as he lifted his entire body weight from the seat. Just as he did, Ron's foot slid on the wet, icy stone and he fell to the ground.

This was a much harder fall than the one he had just endured while riding inside the truck. He landed solidly on his side and most of the wind was punched out of his lungs. It took forty or fifty seconds of gasping before he was able to feel the comfort of breathing once again. Now, to go along with the soreness in his back, he felt a new pain in his ribs. Yet, that was not his worst problem.

As he lost his balance, Ron's right foot was caught between the rock and the front tire of his pickup. Fortunately the weight of his body caused enough leverage to free his foot from the disabling trap, but the pain stretching from his great toe all the way up to his knee was severe. It was obvious that some part of his leg was seriously injured.

Disheveled, writhing in pain, Ron presented a startling contrast to the virgin snow that covered the entire landscape. In took about ten minutes of groaning and rubbing his painful limb for Ron to muster the strength to begin the journey to his cabin, which seemed further away now than it did earlier in the evening when he first left the ski resort.

Trial and error was the only insight that Ron had in deciding how to maneuver his body over the deep snow. He tried crawling. He tried putting weight on the injured leg and limping. He tried hopping on one leg. He finally decided to crawl on his left leg and drag his right leg behind him, like a coyote with a newly discovered animal carcass.

Since the snow was still falling, the moon and stars were missing behind the clouds. Although everything had a white coat, there was little light to brighten the way. The only illumination was from the pickup headlights that were still shining. However, since the truck was facing nose down in the snow, the preponderance of the light was swallowed by the ground. Ron would have to make his way in the dark, over the snow, with a very sore back and unusable leg.

Ron estimated that he was at least a thousand yards from

the front porch of his small cabin. Even under the best of conditions it would be a difficult journey with his injuries, but crawling through several feet of fresh snow and shivering in twenty degrees of arctic air made it an impossible task. His options were to lie down and freeze to death or crawl toward his cabin until exhausted and then freeze to death. He chose the later.

Although you would not say that Ron's life had been fulfilling and worthwhile, he had never been suicidal. He wanted to live, so it is not surprising that he crawled as far as he did. After about twenty minutes, Ron had drug himself about half the distance to his cabin. Although he was afraid to stop for fear that he would never move again, Ron had no choice. Perhaps a two or three minute break would enable him to finish, so he allowed himself to take a rest.

He reclined in the snow, flat on his back staring straight up into the black sky. The rest felt so good that he allowed his eyes to close, just for a minute. He knew that if he went to sleep it would be his final rest. His body was paying the price. Sensation had already departed his toes and fingers and even though he could not see his face, he knew the saliva and tears were frozen like a mudpack on his skin.

However, the combination of being awake for nearly twenty hours, a long day of labor on the Colorado ski slope, the tedious drive over snow-packed mountain roads, and the agony of crawling like a wounded animal had taken their toll. Once Ron closed his eyes, he quickly fell asleep. The Rocky Mountains were about to kill his body just like the Vietnam jungle killed his soul. By now, it was very early

Sunday morning, Christmas Day.

For some reason it is easier to believe in miracles on Christmas. That word-miracle-is the only suitable word to describe what happened next. Just before Ron breathed what would have been the final breath of his life, a large gloved hand seemingly from heaven reached down, grabbed his shoulder, and shook him awake. Returning from the threshold of death takes a moment. Ron's head shuddered quickly as he sought to regain consciousness. As he neared alertness, he began to hear his name, "Ron! Ron! Is that you?"

There were only a handful of people in the whole world who even knew Ron well enough to call him by name and none of them would be here, outside Leadville, Colorado on a frozen Christmas morning, in knee deep snow. The thought that it might be someone in heaven never entered his mind because Ron had no expectation of ever going to heaven and he was too cold for it to be someone from anywhere else. He was still alive somehow, but who was this?

Whoever it was took charge immediately. He lifted Ron to a seated position, surveyed the situation and discovered the injured leg, and then hoisted Ron to his feet. With Ron's right arm over the rescuer's left shoulder, they walked like two men in a three-legged race to the nearby cabin.

The cabin was toasty and the coffee was hot. Ron was still in such a mental fog that he had been unable to identify his savior, but at this point, it mattered little. He was in his own bed, buried under a pile of warm blankets, heated on the inside by the coffee, and now allowed to fall asleep with realistic hope of waking up.

It was approaching one thirty, early on Christmas morning when Ron succumbed to a deep sleep. He suffered from minor frostbite on all of his fingers, toes, and tip of his nose, and it was apparent that he had a broken right leg that would require medical attention whenever circumstances allowed-but he was safe.

He awoke slowly and deliberately after nearly seven hours of sleep. From the amount of light flooding his little cabin, it was apparent that the sun was bright in the sky, an occurrence that is not uncommon after a heavy Rocky Mountain snowfall. In spite of the fact that the cabin was warmer than he usually enjoyed for good sleeping, Ron appreciated the heat. It would take several days before he would take pleasure in cool temperatures again.

Before even moving to sit up, Ron was reminded of his injured leg as a razor-sharp pain shot toward the base of his spine. It was an instant memento of the entire evening's experience. His memory was as clear as a freshly squeegeed window pane, up until he fell asleep in the snow. He had no explanation for how he was transported from his potential frozen grave to his soft feather mattress.

"You finally woke up."

The baritone voice startled Ron and his first thought was to grab something to use for a weapon.

"You looked so comfortable I let you sleep," the voice continued. "How ya feelin'?"

"Who are you?" Ron asked as he began to realize he was in no danger from the stranger.

"You don't recognize me, do you," he responded. "I guess I'm not surprised. It's been a long time."

Ron began to mentally correspond the face before him with those in his memory bank, but without success.

The stranger continued, "You are Ron Milburn of the 2nd Platoon, Company F aren't you? At least that's what I figured out while waiting for you to come home last night. I've been lookin' for you for the better part of six months."

Whoever this stranger was, he was trying to take Ron back to a place and time that he didn't want to go. He had spent the majority of the past three years trying to forget everything about his military experience and he wasn't interested in discussing it with this stranger.

"I'm not surprised you don't remember me. The last time, probably the only time you ever saw me, I wasn't too pretty.

"What's this all about?" Ron asked. The impatience in his voice was obvious.

The stranger hesitated for a moment, as if intentionally building the suspense, and then said, "Ok, I'll tell you. I didn't expect you to remember, but then I didn't expect to find you sleepin' in a snow drift either."

The next forty-five minutes provided the opportunity for the stranger to tell his story to Ron. It was a tale that began with a miracle and ended with a miracle. As the two men talked, they shared cups of stiff coffee brewed in Ron's percolator.

The only previous encounter between them occurred

three years earlier on the outskirts of a Vietnamese village. The stranger's platoon had been ambushed and took heavy casualties. He was one of only four soldiers left alive after the initial attack. They were pinned down by heavy gunfire; they called desperately on the crackling radio for help. It was Ron's platoon that was sent to the rescue.

This type of skirmish happened so frequently during the war that Ron had to admit that he didn't remember this particular battle.

As usual, Ron was one of the first on the scene and he immediately showered the enemy with a stream of gunfire. He noticed a young soldier with his face buried in a muddy ditch, but obviously alive. As soon as the bulk of Ron's platoon arrived on the scene, he called for them to supply cover so he could salvage the injured soldier. With the same reckless abandon that typified Ron's entire military career, Ron half ran and half crawled across the open field, forcefully grabbed the back of the injured man's shirt and drug him to safety. Within minutes, a chopper arrived with reinforcements and medics and they evacuated the injured soldier.

"His name was Christopher Morgan from Fort Wayne, Indiana." At that point, he extended his right arm to shake hands. "Thank you for saving my life!"

Ron accepted his hand but did not respond with a vigorous shake. "You came all they way up here just to tell me that?"

"Hey, it's not that simple. I had to see the man who gave me life. I spent more than two years in the VA and then it took me more than six months to find out who you were and where you live!"

"I figured you died over there, just like the rest of us," replied Ron with a hint of bitterness in his voice.

"No, no," answered Chris, "Quite the opposite.

I fought hard just to live. . . I discovered what life is all about. I get up each day and I'm excited about what God has for me to do. I never know. Just like yesterday. When I got out of bed, I had no idea I'd be draggin' you out of a snow bank. There's a reason I'm alive!"

"There's a reason I'm alive!" Those words stuck in Ron's mind like white glue on construction paper.

"You know, one of the things that kept me alive while I was stuck in the VA was the need to find you and say thanks!" This was the second time Chris had used the word "thanks," but this time he had a slight moistness in his eyes. The need to express gratitude to the man who had saved his life gave him reason enough to endure the pain. "I thought my life was over," he continued, "but then you grabbed me and drug me to the medics. At that moment I knew I wasn't gonna die."

By now, the tears had become contagious. It felt good to know that he had helped someone, even after spending years trying to forget. However, Ron couldn't let go of Chris' statement, "There's a reason I'm alive."

Could that be true for him as well? Is there a reason why Ron survived when so many others didn't? Was it only a coincidence that Chris found him buried in a Colorado snow drift just moments before he died? Ron wasn't sure what it all meant, but for the first time in three years, since that terrible experience in Vietnam, he had a glimpse of a future.

As the bright sun turned the new snow into a glistening marvel, Ron and Chris spent the entire day talking and remembering, laughing and crying. By the time evening shadows began to cover Ron's cabin, he knew that his life would be different. He actually had thoughts about the future, about possible relationships, about all those things he had intentionally avoided. For the first time in years, he felt alive.

It was on a Sunday morning, Christmas Sunday morning, that Ron came alive to a new life.